Books by Jonathan Kellerman

FICTION

ALEX DELAWARE NOVELS

Victims (2012)

Mystery (2011)

Deception (2010)

Evidence (2009)

Bones (2008)

Compulsion (2008)

Obsession (2007)

Gone (2006)

Rage (2005)

Therapy (2004)

A Cold Heart (2003)

The Murder Book (2002)

Flesh and Blood (2001)

Dr. Death (2000)

Monster (1999)

Survival of the Fittest (1997)

The Clinic (1997)

The Web (1996)

Self-Defense (1995)

Bad Love (1994)

Devil's Waltz (1993)

Private Eyes (1992)

Time Bomb (1990)

Silent Partner (1989)

Over the Edge (1987)

Blood Test (1986)

When the Bough Breaks (1985)

OTHER NOVELS

True Detectives (2009)

Capital Crimes (with Faye Kellerman, 2006)

Twisted (2004)

Double Homicide (with Faye Kellerman, 2004)

The Conspiracy Club (2003)

Billy Straight (1998)

The Butcher's Theater (1988)

NONFICTION

With Strings Attached: The Art and Beauty of Vintage Guitars (2008)

Savage Spawn: Reflections on Violent Children (1999)

Helping the Fearful Child (1981)

Psychological Aspects of Childhood Cancer (1980)

FOR CHILDREN, WRITTEN AND ILLUSTRATED

Jonathan Kellerman's ABC of Weird Creatures (1995)

Daddy, Daddy, Can You Touch the Sky? (1994)

THE WEB

THE WEB

THE GRAPHIC NOVEL

JONATHAN KELLERMAN

ADAPTED BY **ANDE PARKS**
ART BY **MICHAEL GAYDOS**

BALLANTINE BOOKS • **NEW YORK**

Published in the United States by Ballantine Books, an imprint of Random House, a division of Random House LLC, a Penguin Random House Company, New York.

BALLANTINE BOOKS and the HOUSE colophon are registered trademarks of Random House LLC.

ISBN 978-0-345-54149-9
eBook ISBN 978-0-345-54150-5

Printed in the United States of America on acid-free paper

www.ballantinebooks.com

9 8 7 6 5 4 3 2 1

First Edition

Text design by Dana Hayward

THE WEB

AS WE PULLED INTO THE HARBOR, THE ISLAND OF ARUK SEEMED AS PRISTINE AS WE HAD BEEN LED TO BELIEVE. A LITTLE SLICE OF PARADISE IN THE SOUTH PACIFIC.

I WOULDN'T HEAR THE STORIES UNTIL AFTER WE'D ARRIVED:

LOCALS, LONG-ENSLAVED BY JAPANESE OCCUPIERS, PICKING UP ANY WEAPON AT HAND AFTER ALLIED BOMBINGS IN WWII . . .

. . . AND CLIMBING THE HILL TOWARD THE HOUSE FULL OF JAPANESE OFFICERS, INTENT ON BLOODY RETRIBUTION.

A CAT-WOMAN, SHRIEKING. ENRAGED.

CHAINED TO HER OWN BED, CLAWING AT THE AIR UNTIL HER HEART EXPLODED.

WHITE WORM PEOPLE, DRAGGING THEIR MISSHAPEN LIMBS THROUGH SINUOUS BANYANS...

...THEIR SKIN *GLOWING* IN THE MOONLIGHT.

DEFORMED FACES *CONTORTING*, THEIR MOUTHS ATTEMPTING *SCREAMS*, BUT MANAGING ONLY FAINT, PITIFUL MOANS.

YOUNG WOMEN MURDERED. BUTCHERED.

THEIR BLOOD AND ORGANS *STAINING* SMOOTH WHITE ROCK NEXT TO A PERFECTLY *WHITE* BEACH.

IF I'D *KNOWN* WHAT WAS WAITING FOR US ON THE ISLAND OF ARUK, I WOULD *NEVER* HAVE BOARDED THE YACHT THAT TOOK US THERE.

I CERTAINLY WOULDN'T HAVE ASKED *ROBIN* TO JOIN ME.

OF COURSE, I **DIDN'T** KNOW. I ONLY KNEW THAT WE HAD BEEN OFFERED WHAT SEEMED LIKE AN **EXTRAORDINARY** OPPORTUNITY.

A LETTER FROM DOCTOR WILSON MORELAND, WHO SAID HE'D READ AN ARTICLE OF MINE IN A PSYCHIATRIC JOURNAL. HE'D ADMIRED MY "SCHOLARLINESS AND COMMON-SENSE THINKING."

A FOUR MONTH STAY ON ARUK, TO HELP THE DOCTOR SORT THROUGH DECADES' WORTH OF CLINICAL DATA. THE DOCTOR'S FILES. A BOOK OR ARTICLE AS THE END RESULT.

ARRIVING AT **ANY** OTHER TIME, IT WOULD HAVE BEEN AN EASY OFFER TO IGNORE.

BUT, ROBIN AND I WERE REBUILDING OUR HOME, AFTER IT HAD BEEN **BURNED** BY A PSYCHOPATH. AND ROBIN WAS **HEALING**.

SEVERE TENDINITIS IN HER WRIST HAD KEPT HER FROM HER INSTRUMENT-MAKING WORKSHOP.

SO, WE'D HEADED OUT, WITH **SPIKE** IN TOW...A LITTLE SEASICK, BUT SEEMING AS EAGER AS WE WERE...

...TO SETTLE INTO OUR NEW, TEMPORARY **HOME** ON ARUK.

THE CAPTAIN SAID SOMEONE WOULD BE ALONG TO PICK US UP...

...JUST AS I SPOTTED THE JEEP. A DRIVER WHO LOOKED TO BE A LOCAL, ALONG WITH A **PASSENGER** WHO SEEMED VERY ANXIOUS TO GREET US.

BEN ROMERO. **WELCOME** TO ARUK.

ALEX DELAWARE. THIS IS ROBIN CASTAGNA... AND SPIKE.

EXCELLENT. SO GLAD YOU'RE HERE. THIS LITTLE GUY IS KIKO.

HIS NAME IS SPIKE, KIKO.

I SHOULD GIVE YOU A PROPER WELCOME: AHUMA NA AHAP. THAT'S OLD PIDGIN FOR "ENJOY OUR HOME."

NOW... LET'S GET YOUR THINGS LOADED. HOW WAS YOUR TRIP?

TIRING BUT GOOD.

THE ISLAND IS BEAUTIFUL.

IT REALLY IS.

DR. MORELAND HAD AN AIR CONDITIONER INSTALLED IN YOUR SUITE, BUT I DOUBT YOU'LL NEED IT.

JANUARY'S ONE OF THE PRETTIEST MONTHS. SOME RAIN BURSTS, BUT IT STAYS AROUND EIGHTY.

LAUGHTER FROM A PAIR OF MEN *CARVING* UP A SHARK THEY'D CAUGHT GRABBED OUR ATTENTION.

I KNEW I WAS TRYING TO NOT LOOK SHOCKED BY THE BLOOD. I ASSUMED THE SAME OF ROBIN.

WELL, WE SHOULD GET GOING.

I'M SURE YOU'RE *ANXIOUS* TO SEE WHERE YOU'LL BE LIVING...MAYBE GET A LITTLE REST.

"ON THE WAY TO DR. MORELAND'S HOME..."

"...I CAN SHOW YOU SOME OF THE LOCAL SIGHTS."

BEN POINTED OUT THE SIGHTS AS WE DROVE.

DR. MORELAND, HE SAID, WANTED TO GREET US *PERSONALLY*, BUT HAD TO TREAT SOME CHILDREN WHO'D BEEN STUNG BY JELLYFISH.

WE DROVE THROUGH THE ISLAND'S BUSINESS DISTRICT. MOST OF THE BUILDINGS WERE *CLOSED*, INCLUDING THE GAS STATION.

ARUK WAS A U.S. TERRITORY, BUT IT COULD HAVE BEEN *ANYWHERE* IN THE DEVELOPING WORLD.

HAVE YOU LIVED **HERE** YOUR WHOLE LIFE?

YEAH, EXCEPT FOR COAST GUARD AND NURSING SCHOOL IN HAWAII. MET MY WIFE THERE.

SHE'S A CHINESE GIRL. WE HAVE FOUR KIDS.

WHERE'S THE JUNGLE?

NOT **REALLY** MUCH JUNGLE. I MEAN, THERE'RE NO WILD ANIMALS OR ANYTHING.

THE BANYANS DO GET THICK ON THE EAST SIDE. NEAR DR. MORELAND'S PLACE.

THE ROAD CHANGED FROM GRAVEL TO SMOOTH ASPHALT AS WE ENTERED THE MORELAND ESTATE.

NOT **EVERYONE** ON ARUK WAS IMPOVERISHED.

THE JAPANESE ARMY BUILT THE HOUSE IN 1919. THIS WAS THEIR HEADQUARTERS.

THE WHOLE PLACE IS ROCK SOLID. BIGGEST STRUCTURE ON THE ISLAND, OUTSIDE OF THE NAVAL BASE.

BEN OPENED THE FRONT DOOR WITHOUT A KEY.

IT HAD BEEN A LONG TIME SINCE I'D SEEN A DOOR LEFT UNLOCKED IN L.A.

THE ESTATE IS PRETTY LARGE. SEVEN HUNDRED ACRES, GIVE OR TAKE.

OVER A SQUARE MILE. BIG CHUNK OF A SEVEN-BY-ONE-MILE ISLAND.

THE HOUSE IS JUST LOVELY.

YEAH... QUITE A PLACE.

AH...GOOD. YOU SHOULD MEET GLADYS MEDINA, GOURMET CHEF AND EXECUTIVE HOUSEKEEPER, AND HER DAUGHTER, CHERYL.

DR. ALEX DELAWARE AND MS. ROBIN CASTAGNA.

PLEASE. WE COOK AND CLEAN. NICE TO MEET YOU.

FALSE MODESTY.

COME ON...I'LL SHOW YOU YOUR ROOMS.

MISTER ROMERO...?

OH...YES, CARL. THIS IS CARL SLEET, THE PROPERTY'S GARDENER.

WOULD YOU PLEASE SEE THAT OUR GUESTS' THINGS GET TO THEIR ROOMS? THE JEEP IS OUT FRONT.

EVERYONE'S BEEN WITH DR. BILL A LONG TIME.

GLADYS HAS BEEN WITH HIM SINCE HE LEFT THE NAVY. SHE USED TO WORK FOR THE COMMANDER AT THE BASE.

SHE GOT SCRUB TYPHUS. THE NAVY FIRED HER. BILL HIRED HER RIGHT AWAY. HER DAUGHTER CHERYL IS A BIT...SLOW.

AND... HERE WE ARE...

MY GOD... LOOK AT THAT VIEW.

YEAH...THE JAPANESE MILITARY GOVERNOR WANTED TO BE KING OF THE MOUNTAIN.

THAT PEAK IS THE **HIGHEST** POINT ON THE ISLAND.

THE JAPANESE FIGURED THE MOUNTAINS GAVE THEM A NATURAL BARRIER FROM AN EASTERN LAND ASSAULT.

WE PASSED THE SLAVE BARRACKS ON THE WAY UP.

WHEN MCARTHUR TOOK THE ISLAND, THE SLAVES **TURNED** ON THE JAPANESE. I GUESS IT GOT PRETTY UGLY.

UMM... YOU **CAN** DRINK THE WATER. CARBON FILTERS ON ALL THE CISTERNS.

AND ALL OUR FRUITS AND VEGETABLES ARE **ORGANIC**. DR. BILL GROWS IT ALL HIMSELF.

YOUR STUFF WILL BE BROUGHT UP LATER. ANYTHING **ELSE** I CAN DO FOR YOU?

WE SEEM TO HAVE EVERYTHING. THANKS.

GREAT. DINNER'S AT SIX. DRESS COMFORTABLY.

AS ROBIN FRESHENED UP IN THE BATHROOM, I FOUND A **NOTE** LEFT BY OUR HOST.

Home is the sailor, home from sea,
And the hunter home from the hill.
—R. L. Stevenson

Please make my home yours.
WWM

"DON'T **WORRY.** I CHECKED THE LINES OF SIGHT FROM THE WINDOWS."

NO ONE CAN SEE IN.

HOW NICE. GOD, YOU'RE BEAUTIFUL.

LOVE YOU.

LOVE YOU **BACK.** THIS IS GOING TO BE **WONDER-FUL.**

I WOKE A FEW HOURS LATER, TO A SOUND FROM NEXT DOOR. I COULDN'T MAKE OUT THE WORDS, BUT THE **TONE** WAS UNMISTAKABLE.

TWO PEOPLE ARGUING WITH THAT GRINDING RELENTLESSNESS THAT SAID THEY'D HAD **LONG** PRACTICE.

WHAT TIME IS IT, ALEX?

FIVE-FORTY.

TWENTY MINUTES TO DINNER. MAYBE I'LL TAKE ANOTHER QUICK BATH.

HOW'S THE WRIST FEEL?

BETTER, ACTUALLY. ALL THE WARM AIR. AND DOING NOTHING FOR A FEW DAYS.

THE POWER OF POSITIVE **NOTHING.**

ALEX, ROBIN. YOU'RE **RIGHT** ON TIME. I'D LIKE YOU TO MEET YOUR NEIGHBORS.

THEY SMILED. HIS MORE **FORCED** THAN HERS. A HALF HOUR EARLIER, THEY'D BEEN ASSAULTING EACH OTHER WITH WORDS.

DR. AND MRS. DELAWARE, I PRESUME?

ROBIN CASTAGNA AND ALEX DELAWARE.

JO PICKER, LYMAN PICKER. **DR.** JO PICKER AND LYMAN PICKER.

ACTUALLY, IT'S **DR.** LYMAN PICKER, TOO, BUT WHO CARES ABOUT THAT NONSENSE.

GLAD YOU'RE HERE. ROUND OUT THE DINNER TABLE. MAKE UP FOR OUR **HOST'S** ABSENCE.

THE MAN IS ALL **WORK**, NO PLAY. WHEN HE SLEEPS, I'LL NEVER KNOW.

ARE YOU DOING RESEARCH WITH DR. MORELAND?

NOT I. MY FIELD IS TROPICAL SPORES.

I RARELY VENTURE FAR FROM THE EQUATOR.

KEEPING THE DISTAFF SIDE COMPANY. DR. JO HERE IS AN **ESTEEMED** METEOROLOGIST.

I STUDY WIND PATTERNS.

I UNDERSTAND OUR HOST WILL BE LATE, AS USUAL. MAY AS WELL TAKE OUR SEATS.

I'LL SHOW THEM TO THE DINING ROOM. DRINKS, BEN?

BOURBON, STRAIGHT UP FOR ME.

SO YOU'RE HERE TO WORK WITH THE OLD MAN. HE'S LUCKY TO GET YOU. YOU WOULDN'T FIND A **SERIOUS** SCIENTIST ON THIS DIRT SPECK.

NO OFFENSE.

DID YOU KNOW THERE WERE NO PEOPLE HERE UNTIL THE SPANISH BROUGHT THEM TO GROW SUGAR?

THEN THE **GERMANS,** AND THE **JAPANESE.** THEN THE "NIGHT OF THE LONG KNIVES." NO MORE OUTSIDERS AFTER **THAT.**

PRESENT COMPANY **EXCLUDED,** OF COURSE.

GOD, WHERE'S THAT **DRINK?**

"I'M SURE BEN IS ON HIS WAY, LYMAN. IN THE **MEANTIME...**"

...I DOUBT YOU'LL DIE OF THIRST.

HELLO. I'M **PAM.** DOCTOR MORELAND'S DAUGHTER.

NICE TO MEET YOU BOTH. SORRY I'M **LATE.** DAD SHOULD BE HERE SHORTLY.

GLADYS HAS DONE A NICE CHICKEN KIEV. DAD'S VEGETARIAN, BUT HE TOLERATES US BARBARIANS.

SHALL I OPEN **ANOTHER** BOTTLE, DR. PICKER?

AN HOUR INTO THE MEAL, LYMAN HAD CONSUMED AS MUCH WHISKEY AS FOOD. AS HE DRANK, HE BECAME EVEN **MORE** INSUFFERABLE.

NO THANK YOU, AMIGO. BETTER KEEP MY WITS. I'M **FLYING** TOMORROW.

YES, JO... I'M GOING AHEAD WITH IT. ONE OF THE PLANES OWNED BY A MAN NAMED AMALFI.

THE MISSUS HERE IS **NERVOUS** ABOUT IT, BUT I EXAMINED THE PLANES MYSELF. BEEN BUZZING JUNGLES FOR **YEARS.**

WE'RE GOING OUT TO SEE **YOUR** POOR EXCUSE FOR ONE IN THE MORNING. TAKE SOME PICTURES.

I'M NOT SURE THAT'S A GOOD IDEA, DR. PICKER.

YOU'LL RISK FLYING OVER THE NAVAL BASE, AND THOSE PLANES AREN'T—

EVERYONE SO **CONCERNED** ABOUT ME. TOUCHING.

LYMAN... **PLEASE**—

FONTS OF HUMAN KINDNESS TO MY **FACE,** BUT BEHIND MY BACK: DRUNKEN BUFFOON.

DAMN THIS PLACE!

VOLCANOES EJACULATING, THEN DROPPING DEAD. EVERYTHING SLOWLY **SINKING.** ENTROPY.

WHAT A PERFECT METAPHOR.

EVERYTHING SINKS.

SO...

...EVERYTHING WAS **EXCELLENT**. GLADYS IS REALLY TALENTED.

SHE COOKS VEGETARIAN FOR YOUR FATHER?

YES. SHE'S VERY CREATIVE. NOT THAT DAD EVER GETS TO DINNER ON TIME TO ENJOY IT.

I KEEP **TELLING** HIM HE NEEDS TO TAKE BETTER CARE OF HIMSELF.

"YES..."

...AND I KEEP IGNORING HER, **STUBBORN MULE** THAT I AM.

AN HOUR AND A HALF LATER, IT WAS JUST ME AND MORELAND. HIS EYES WERE BLUE... SAD AND, MORE THAN ANYTHING...TIRED.

HE ASKED ME TO CALL HIM BILL. I TOLD HIM TO CALL ME ALEX.

HOW ARE YOUR ACCOMMODATIONS?

GREAT. THANKS FOR EVERYTHING.

OF COURSE. WHAT DID YOU THINK OF MY STEVENSON QUOTE?

NICE TOUCH. GREAT WRITER.

YES. AND A GREAT THINKER. THE GREAT THINKERS HAVE SO MUCH TO OFFER.

I HAVE HIGH HOPES FOR OUR PROJECT, ALEX. WHO KNOWS WHAT WILL EMERGE WHEN WE DIG INTO THE DATA. WHAT PATTERNS...

MENTAL HEALTH PROBLEMS ALWAYS SEEM TO POSE THE GREATEST PUZZLES.

AND I'VE SEEN SOME FASCINATING CASES. FOR EXAMPLE, YEARS AGO I ENCOUNTERED A CASE OF— I SUPPOSE THE CLOSEST LABEL WOULD BE...LYCANTHROPY.

A WOLF-MAN?

A CAT WOMAN. HAVE YOU SEEN THAT?

DURING MY TRAINING I SAW SCHIZOPHRENICS WITH **TRANSITORY** ANIMAL HALLUCINATIONS.

THIS WAS **MORE** THAN TRANSITORY. THIRTY-YEAR-OLD WOMAN, QUITE ATTRACTIVE, SWEET NATURE, UNTIL...

SHORTLY AFTER HER THIRTY-FIRST BIRTHDAY, SHE STARTED CHASING MICE. MEWING, LICKING HERSELF."

"EATING RAW MEAT. THAT'S WHAT FINALLY BROUGHT HER TO ME: INTESTINAL PARASITES."

"SHE HAD **ACUTE** SPELLS, LASTING LONGER AS TIME WENT ON."

"**INTERESTING** FROM A DIAGNOSTIC STANDPOINT, WOULDN'T YOU SAY?"

SHE BECAME QUITE **AGGRESSIVE**, TO THE POINT WHERE HER HUSBAND TIED HER UP IN HER ROOM.

SHE SCREAMED OUT ONE NIGHT— A CRI DU CHAT—CAT'S CRY. THE HUSBAND FOUND HER...**DEAD**.

WHAT WAS HER **RELATIONSHIP** WITH HER HUSBAND LIKE?

IS THERE ANY **PARTICULAR** REASON YOU ASK THAT?

I'M A **PSYCHOLOGIST.**

INDEED.

THERE WERE OTHER WOMEN. LOTS OF THEM. THE HUSBAND CONFESSED EVERYTHING ON HIS DEATHBED. LUNG CANCER HAD RAVAGED HIS CHEST.

GUILT IS A GREAT MOTIVATOR, ALEX.

WAS SHE TIED UP THE NIGHT SHE DIED?

YES.

PERHAPS SOMETHING FRIGHTENED OR UPSET HER. AN ESPECIALLY **SEVERE** HALLUCINATION. A NIGHTMARE, OR...

"...SOMETHING REAL."

"MAYBE HER DON JUAN HUSBAND TOOK UP WITH ANOTHER WOMAN *BEFORE* SHE DIED."

"TIED UP AT NIGHT, BUT THE HUSBAND AND THE GIRLFRIEND WERE IN THE NEXT ROOM?"

"DID THEY MAKE LOVE IN *FRONT* OF HER?"

MY, MY. YOU ARE A *REMARKABLE* YOUNG MAN.

JUST GUESSING.

VERY IMPRESSIVE. I HAVE MANY MORE CASES, ALEX. SO MANY MORE. I'M SO GLAD YOU'RE HERE TO *HELP.*

WHENEVER YOU AND ROBIN ARE READY TOMORROW...

"...I'LL TAKE YOU ON A *FULL* TOUR."

THESE PAINTINGS ARE NICE.

OH, *THOSE*. THEY WERE DONE BY MY LATE WIFE.

BY THE WAY, I HEARD ABOUT LYMAN'S BEHAVIOR AT DINNER. I APOLOGIZE.

NO BIG DEAL.

DID YOU HEAR ABOUT THEIR *FLIGHT*?

THEY'RE TAKING A PLANE OWNED BY SOMEONE CALLED AMALFI OUT OVER THE BANYANS.

GOOD *LORD*. THOSE ARE JUNK HEAPS.

I MUST HAVE A WORD WITH LYMAN... NOT THAT *MY* OPINION WILL *CHANGE* HIS MIND.

NOW, COME THIS WAY, PLEASE. LET'S HAVE A LOOK...

...AT MY *GARDENS*.

IT'S WONDERFUL, BILL. **AMAZING.**

THANK YOU, DEAR. ACTUALLY, THERE'S ANOTHER... **COLLECTION** I'M QUITE PROUD OF.

ARE EITHER OF YOU...

"...SQUEAMISH?"

WELCOME TO MY LITTLE ZOO.

I'VE ALWAYS BEEN INTERESTED IN **NATURAL PREDATION.** SPINELESS CREATURES CAN PROVIDE INCREDIBLE PEST CONTROL.

SO...YOU'RE SURE YOU WANT TO SEE THEM MORE... UP **CLOSE?**

I'M READY. WHEN I WAS A KID I HAD A TARANTULA AS A PET.

REALLY? I DIDN'T KNOW THAT.

NEITHER DID MY **MOTHER,** UNTIL SHE FOUND IT IN THE SHOEBOX IN MY CLOSET.

AUSTRALIAN GARDEN WOLF, COUSIN OF YOUR CHILDHOOD PET. LIKE **TARANTULA**, THEY BURROW AND WAIT.

WOULD YOU LIKE TO **HOLD** HER?

A NEW FRIEND, GINA.

SHE'S **CUTE**.

HOLD HER AS LONG AS YOU LIKE, DEAR. WHEN YOU'RE **READY**, THOUGH...

"...THERE'S **LOTS** MORE TO SEE."

ROW AFTER ROW. AQUARIUM AFTER AQUARIUM. AN **AMAZING** COLLECTION.

EVERY TYPE OF SPIDER. A STICK-LIKE AUSTRALIAN HYGROPODA. A BORNEAN JUMPER WHOSE FACE REMINDED ME OF A WISE OLD MAN.

AND, OF COURSE, THE **BIGGEST** TARANTULA I'D EVER SEEN.

NOW, HERE'S A **BRILLIANT** EXAMPLE OF NATURAL PEST CONTROL.

IF IT WEREN'T FOR PUBLIC PREJUDICE, **THIS** BEAUTY COULD BE TRAINED TO CLEAR HOMES OF RATS.

I TRIED **NOT** TO MOVE AWAY FROM THE SPIDER, AND ALMOST SUCCEEDED.

THIS IS EMMA AND SHE'S **SPOILED**.

THIS IS THE TARANTULA OF B-MOVIES, BUT SHE'S REALLY A GRAMMOSTOLA, FROM THE AMAZON.

I STAY AWAY FROM BUTTERFLIES AND MOTHS. TOO SHORT-LIVED AND THEY NEED FLYING ROOM TO BE TRULY HAPPY.

ALL MY GUESTS ADAPT WELL TO CLOSE QUARTERS AND...

FORGIVE ME. I'M PROBABLY BORING YOU TO TEARS.

NO. THEY'RE ALL SO... IMPRESSIVE.

YOU'RE TOO KIND. YOU HUMOR ME. COME...JUST ONE MORE.

MY BRONTOSAURUS. HIS ANCESTORS COEXISTED WITH THE DINOSAURS.

THE GIANT CENTIPEDE OF EAST ASIA.

I NOTICED EVEN MORELAND DIDN'T SEEMED TO WANT TO HANDLE THIS ONE. I FELL BACK A FULL STEP.

MORE VENOMOUS THAN MOST SPIDERS.

I HAVEN'T NAMED HIM YET. HAVEN'T QUITE TRAINED HIM TO LOVE ME.

LATER, WE WERE HEADED TO THE BEACH WHEN LYMAN PICKER FLAGGED US DOWN.

HE WANTED A RIDE TO THE ISLAND'S AIRSTRIP. APPARENTLY, NO ONE HAD BEEN ABLE TO TALK HIM OUT OF FLYING.

WATCH FOR POT-HOLES. **TERRIBLE** SHOCKS ON THIS THING.

HOW ARE YOU LIKING THE OLD PLANTATION? NOTICE THE ROTARY PHONES. **GOD**... IT'S A **WONDER** IT'S NOT TWO CANS AND A STRING.

IF YOU DON'T **LIKE** IT, WHY STAY?

WE DO LIKE IT.

EXCELLENT QUESTION, MS. CRAFTSPERSON. IF IT WERE UP TO ME, WE WOULD **NOT** BE STAYING.

WE DROVE THE REST OF THE WAY IN UNCOMFORTABLE SILENCE.

LYMAN DIRECTED ME TOWARD A DESOLATE PIECE OF LAND THAT SERVED AS THE ISLAND'S AIRSTRIP. NO RUNWAY. JUST A PATCH OF FLAT GROUND.

IT WAS **EASY** TO SEE WHY EVERYONE BUT LYMAN PICKER THOUGHT THIS FLIGHT WAS A BAD IDEA.

THE PLANE LOOKED TO BE AS **OLD** AS LYMAN HIMSELF, AND ABOUT AS WELL-MAINTAINED.

WHERE'S YOUR FATHER, SKIP? WE'RE RENTING A PLANE.

HE'S 'ROUND.

POOR JO. SHE'S **SCARED** TO DEATH.

MISTER PICKER.

GOT HER GREASED AND TUNED UP FOR YA.

YOU MUST BE THE DOCTOR'S NEW GUESTS.

TREATIN' YOU **GOOD**?

VERY MUCH SO.

YEAH...WELL, DON'T **COUNT** ON IT. YOU WANNA GO UP, **TOO**?

NO. NO THANKS.

MAYBE SOME OTHER TIME.

HARRY AMALFI TURNED TO THE LYMANS AND HIS PLANE, AND I HIT THE GAS.

DRIVING PAST THE HOUSE, I NOTICED THE BLEACHED SHARK'S JAWS THAT LINED THE MOLDING OF THE FRONT DOOR.

I HATE LEAVING JO THERE LIKE THAT.

SO DO I, BUT I DIDN'T SEE ANY **OPTIONS**.

LET'S FIND THAT BEACH. A SWIM WILL HELP **BOTH** OF US FEEL BETTER.

AS WE APPROACHED THE LOCAL RESTAURANT, THE CHOP SUEY PALACE, I SAW A MAN SEATED OUTSIDE.

HE FLAGGED US DOWN. *AMERICAN*, FROM THE DOCK SHOES TO THE SLICK HAIRCUT.

TOM CREEDMAN. I HEARD THE NEW AMERICANS WERE IN TOWN. **L.A.**, RIGHT?

RIGHT.

NEW YORK. BEFORE THAT, D.C. USED TO WORK IN THE NEWS BUSINESS.

C'MON IN... *JOIN ME FOR A BEER.*

BOTH OF US WANTED TO GET TO THE BEACH, BUT WE ACCEPTED CREEDMAN'S INVITATION.

SMALL ISLAND. NO POINT ANNOYING PEOPLE SO EARLY IN OUR STAY.

JACQUI!

THE NEW GUESTS UP AT KNIFE CASTLE. A ROUND FOR EVERYONE.

KNIFE CASTLE?

LOCAL NICKNAME FOR YOUR LODGINGS? DIDN'T YOU KNOW? THE JAPANESE USED TO USE THE LOCALS AS SLAVES.

DURING MAC-ARTHUR'S BOMBINGS, THE SLAVES GOT EVEN. KNIFE CASTLE.

I DID A LOT OF RESEARCH WHEN I GOT TO THE ISLAND. OLD HABITS.

THANKS, JACQUI. KEEP THE BUCK.

SO, WHAT BROUGHT YOU TO ARUK?

WORKING ON A BOOK. NONFICTION. LIFE CHANGES, ISOLATION, THE WHOLE ISLAND MYSTIQUE THING.

CAN'T REALLY SAY MORE.

WHAT BRINGS *YOU* TWO HERE? HOW LONG ARE YOU STAYING?

I'M HELPING DR. MORELAND ORGANIZE HIS DATA. IT'LL PROBABLY TAKE A FEW MONTHS.

YOU'RE A PSYCHOLOGIST, *RIGHT?* MORELAND WANTS HELP ANALYZING HIS PATIENTS PSYCHOLOGICALLY?

WE'RE STILL DISCUSSING THE *SPECIFICS.*

SO, WHERE DO YOU LIVE, TOM?

JUST UP THERE. SPENT A FEW DAYS AT MORELAND'S BUT COULDN'T TAKE IT.

TOO INTENSE. HE'S *SOMETHING,* ISN'T HE?

HE SEEMS VERY *DEDICATED.*

YEAH. EASY TO BE DEDICATED WHEN YOU'RE *LOADED.*

HIS FATHER WAS A BIG SAN FRANCISCO INVESTMENT HONCHO. *BIG BUCKS.*

HEY... MORE POWER TO HIM, TRYING TO *SAVE* THIS HUNK OF ROCK.

A *TRUE* LOST CAUSE.

ONCE THE NAVY DECIDES TO LEAVE THE BASE, THIS WHOLE ISLAND WILL **WITHER** UP AND **DIE.**

THEY'VE BLOCKADED THE MAIN ROAD TO THE BASE ALREADY.

THE NAVY BLOCKADED THE ROAD TO THEIR OWN BASE? WHY WOULD THEY CONTRIBUTE TO THE ISLAND'S DECLINE LIKE THAT?

TRUST ME...THEY HAD **GOOD** REASON.

PUBLIC SAFETY. LOCAL GIRL'S BODY FOUND ON THE BEACH HALF A YEAR AGO.

RAPED AND MANGLED PRETTY BAD.

MORELAND CAN—UHH—**TELL** YOU ABOUT IT. HE DID THE AUTOPSY.

SOME OF THE LOCAL YOUNG BLOODS GOT **WORKED** UP. SOMEONE SUSPECTED A SAILOR.

HEADED TO THE BASE TO...**TALK** ABOUT IT. A LITTLE CIVIL UNREST. THE BLOCK—

AN EXPLOSION IN THE DISTANCE CUT CREEDMAN OFF. A BIG ONE.

DAMN.

ROBIN AND I HAD THE **SAME** THOUGHT AS SOON AS WE HEARD THE BLAST: LYMAN PICKER AND HIS DAMNED FLIGHT.

THEN WE BOTH THOUGHT OF **JO**.

IT'S A GOOD CRAFT.

WAS.

SHIT. STUPID BASTARD PROBABLY **FLOODED** IT.

WAS IT THE PLANE?

MUST'VE **FLOODED** IT. I'M TELLING YA, IT WAS A **GOOD** CRAFT!

OH, GOD. POOR **JO**. SHE DIDN'T WANT TO GO. SHE—

"NO..."

...I DIDN'T.

WE HAD A **FIGHT**. I WAS PLANNING TO GO BUT I GOT **SCARED**.

I LET HIM GO UP THERE ALONE...

WE GOT JO BACK TO THE HOUSE. ROBIN, GLADYS AND PAM ESCORTED HER TO HER ROOM.

NO SOUNDS CAME FROM THE OTHER SIDE OF THE WALL NOW.

HE WASN'T MR. **CHARM**, BUT TO GO LIKE THAT.

HOW'S JO?

WIPED OUT. SHE WAS TRYING TO GET A CALL THROUGH TO HIS FAMILY.

I KNOW IT'S **TRITE**, BUT ONE MOMENT YOU'RE TALKING TO SOMEONE, THE NEXT THEY'RE **GONE**.

HOW'RE **YOU** DOING? WITH ALL THIS... **VACATION**.

HA...IS **THAT** WHAT THIS IS?

I'M **FINE**. ASSUMING WE'VE USED UP ALL THE BAD VIBES, NOTHING BUT **SUNSHINE** AND **SWEETNESS** AHEAD.

YEAH. WANT TO TRY **DIVING** AGAIN TOMORROW?

MAYBE.

ANYTHING THAT SOUNDS GOOD, LET ME KNOW. I WANT THIS TO BE **GOOD** FOR YOU.

FOR SOME REASON, AFTER **ALL** THESE YEARS, I STILL FEEL I NEED TO COURT YOU.

I KNOW THAT. DON'T STOP.

ALEX?

'MORNING. BILL CALLED EARLY. YOU SLEPT THROUGH IT.

CHECKING ON US **AFTER**...LYMAN AND EVERYTHING. HE'S ANXIOUS TO SHOW US OUR WORK SPACES...

"...WHENEVER YOU'RE READY FOR **ANOTHER** TOUR."

YOUR ATELIER, DEAR. I HOPE IT WILL **SUFFICE**.

I **KNOW** YOU'RE NOT CARVING RIGHT NOW, BUT ALEX TOLD ME HOW **GIFTED** YOU ARE.

IT'S **AMAZING**. EVERYTHING IS SO NICE. SO **NEW**.

I'M SO GLAD YOU'RE **PLEASED**. USE IT WHENEVER YOU FEEL READY, OF COURSE.

NOW THEN, ALEX, ARE YOU PREPARED TO DISCOVER HOW TRULY DISORGANIZED I AM?

"SHE'D GONE THERE FOR A VACATION."

"I WAS BUSY WITH PATIENTS. SHE WAS A STRONG SWIMMER, BUT GOT CAUGHT UP IN A RIPTIDE."

SHE WAS *LOVELY*. SHE SMILED, BUT THERE WAS SOMETHING ABOUT HER POSTURE. A SAD, ALMOST *RESIGNED* QUALITY.

A FEW MOMENTS AFTER I HANDED BILL THE PHOTO OF HIS WIFE, HE WAS SHOWING ME MY NEW OFFICE.

VERY NICE.

YES, WELL, SO FAR...

...YOU'VE ONLY SEEN THE **ORGANIZED** PORTION.

AS YOU CAN SEE, I'VE BEEN **WAITING** FOR YOU.

SHAMEFUL, ISN'T IT? I MUST ADMIT, IT'S MOSTLY RANDOM. I TRIED TO ALPHABETIZE A FEW TIMES, BUT...

I DON'T EXPECT **MIRACLES.** SKIM, PERUSE, **WHATEVER,** TELL ME IF ANYTHING JUMPS OUT AT YOU.

I'VE ALWAYS TRIED TO INCLUDE PSYCHOLOGICAL AND SOCIAL DATA...

WELL... LET'S DIG IN **TOGETHER.**

AN HOUR LATER, WE WERE DUG IN. BILL FLIPPED THROUGH FILES, HIS EYES SIFTING THROUGH THE NOTES OF CASES AND PATIENTS LONG GONE.

OF ALL THINGS...

THIS WASN'T ON ARUK, BUT IT WAS A CASE OF MINE.

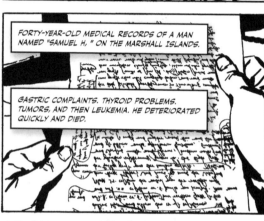

FORTY-YEAR-OLD MEDICAL RECORDS OF A MAN NAMED "SAMUEL H.," ON THE MARSHALL ISLANDS.

GASTRIC COMPLAINTS. THYROID PROBLEMS. TUMORS, AND THEN LEUKEMIA. HE DETERIORATED QUICKLY AND DIED.

AREN'T THE MARSHALL ISLANDS CLOSE TO KOREA?

YES. I WAS STATIONED THERE AFTER THE WAR. ANY THOUGHTS ON THE CASE?

SOUNDS LIKE RADIATION POISONING. THIS WOULD BE NEAR THE BIKINI ATOLL, RIGHT? NUCLEAR TESTS AFTER WWII.

THE WINDS SHIFTED, POLLUTING NEARBY ISLANDS.

YES.

TWENTY-THREE BLASTS BETWEEN '46 AND '48. EVERYTHING FROM A-BOMBS...

...TO THE FIRST HYDROGEN WEAPON. THE DUST BLANKETED SEVERAL OF THE ATOLLS. CHILDREN PLAYED IN IT. BREATHED IN THE DUST.

SHIFTING WINDS. I BELIEVED THAT FOR A LONG TIME...

HUMAN **GUINEA PIGS.** LEUKEMIAS, LYMPHOMAS, THY- ROID DISORDERS. AND BIRTH DEFECTS: RETARDATION, LIMBLESS BABIES.

GOD...WE CALLED THEM "JELLYFISH."

WE **COMPENSATED** THE POOR DEVILS. TWENTY-FIVE THOUSAND DOLLARS A VICTIM. I TOOK PART IN THE PROGRAM.

TWENTY-FIVE THOUSAND DOLLARS PER **LIFE.** AN ACTUARIAL **TRIUMPH.**

AFTER I FIGURED OUT WHAT THE BLAST HAD DONE, I PUT IN FOR EXTENDED STAY. TRIED TO DO WHAT I COULD FOR THE PEOPLE.

IT WASN'T **MUCH.**

ALEX, I **READ** YOUR ARTICLES ON PAIN CONTROL. SCIENTIFIC YET **COMPASSIONATE.** I READ THEM **ALL.**

IT'S ONE OF THE REASONS I FELT YOU MIGHT **UNDERSTAND.**

UNDERSTAND WHAT, BILL?

WHY A CRAZY OLD MAN SUDDENLY WANTS TO **ORGANIZE** HIS LIFE.

ONE HOUR AND A DOZEN ROUTINE CASE FILES LATER, I DECIDED TO BRING UP TOM CREEDMAN.

I TOLD BILL WHAT CREEDMAN HAD SAID ABOUT THE **MURDER**, AND THE SOCIAL UNREST THAT FOLLOWED.

HE ALSO SAID HE LIVED **HERE** FOR A SHORT TIME.

OH, **INDEED**. BEN FOUND HIM **SNOOPING** AROUND IN MY OFFICE.

AFTERWARD, HE **INSULTED** BEN. I WON'T **TOLERATE** THAT. I ORDERED HIM OFF THE GROUNDS.

NOW HE DELIGHTS IN ACCENTUATING THE NEGATIVE, ABOUT **ME** AND **ARUK**.

HE ALSO SAID THAT YOU DID THE AUTOPSY. DO YOU **AGREE** THAT IT MIGHT HAVE BEEN A SAILOR?

I'M GROWING A BIT **CONCERNED**, ALEX.

PICKER'S **ACCIDENT**, AND NOW **THIS**. YOU COULD EASILY BE THINKING ARUK IS A **TERRIBLE** PLACE. IT'S NOT.

YES, THE **MURDER** WAS TERRIBLE, BUT...

YOU **DESERVE** TO KNOW THE WHOLE TRUTH.

I'LL BE RIGHT BACK.

BILL RETURNED WITH A COPY OF THE POLICE FILE. THE VICTIM WAS A TWENTY-FOUR-YEAR-OLD WOMAN: ANNEMARIE VALDOS.

ON ARUK FOR TWO YEARS. SHE'D BEEN A COCKTAIL WAITRESS. HAD SOCIALIZED WITH NAVY MEN.

YOU MIGHT NOT WANT TO. PHOTO-GRAPHS.

I THOUGHT ABOUT IT...

...AND FLIPPED ANYWAY.

Dennis:
You may want to keep this private.

WWM Postmortem mutilation
A. The left leg has been severed c the patellar joint.
B. The left femur has been three places, with a con bone marrow removed.
C. A deep 26 cm. long wound extends fr sternum.
D. Disembowel small and l region, ob are intac these

THE SHOTS WEREN'T ANY WORSE THAN SOME OF THE ONES MILO HAD SHOWN ME, WHICH IS TO SAY THEY'D BE ADDITIONS TO MY NIGHTMARE FILE.

39

CONTRARY TO WHAT CREEDMAN HAD SAID, THERE'D BEEN *NO* RAPE.

I SHUT THE FILE AND TOOK A SLOW BREATH, TRYING TO SETTLE MY STOMACH.

I'M *SORRY.* I WANT YOU TO SEE THAT I'M NOT CONCEALING ANYTHING.

THE KILLER WAS NEVER CAUGHT?

UNFORTUNATELY NOT.

ARUK'S POLICE CHIEF, DENNIS LAURENT, IS A *GOOD* MAN. WE *AGREED* IT PROBABLY WASN'T A LOCAL.

HE TRIED TO QUESTION SOME SAILORS, BUT COULD NEVER GET ACCESS TO THE BASE.

HE ASKED ME TO KEEP THE FILE, TO SEE IF I MIGHT COME UP WITH ANYTHING. I *HAVEN'T.*

ANY *SUGGESTIONS?*

NOT YOUR *TYPICAL* SADISTIC MURDER. ORGAN THEFT...IT'S *GHOULISH.* ALMOST RITUALISTIC.

YES...I WAS REMINDED OF *CANNIBALISTIC* RITUALS.

YOUR NOTES SUGGESTED TO LAURENT THAT HE SHOULD KEEP THE DETAILS TO HIMSELF. WHY?

TEMPERS WERE RUNNING HIGH. RUMORS...

I DIDN'T THINK WORD OF A CANNIBAL SAILOR WOULD HELP ANYTHING.

NO ONE KNOWS, ALEX, OTHER THAN YOU, DENNIS, AND MYSELF.

I KNOW I CAN TRUST YOU TO KEEP IT TO YOURSELF.

WHAT ABOUT THE BLOCKADE? DID LOCALS STORM THE BASE?

IT WAS HARDLY A STORM. A FEW DRUNK YOUNG MEN.

THE BLOCKADE... I FEAR IT MAY BE THE FIRST STEP OF CLOSING THE BASE.

IF THE NAVY GOES, THE WHOLE ISLAND WILL FOLLOW.

I TRY NOT TO BE HOPELESS. JUST ONE BIG INVESTMENT HERE COULD SAVE ARUK.

I HAVE AN... ACQUAINTANCE IN CONGRESS. SENATOR HOFFMAN. I'VE TRIED TO GET HIM TO SEE THE POSSIBILITIES HERE.

I'VE HEARD OF HIM. IS HE SYMPATHETIC?

YOU CAN JUDGE FOR YOURSELF, SON.

WE'VE ALL BEEN INVITED TO DINE WITH HIM AT THE BASE TOMORROW NIGHT.

THAT AFTERNOON, ROBIN AND I **FINALLY MADE** IT TO THE BEACH.

THE WATER WAS AS **PRISTINE** AS WE'D BEEN PROMISED. AFTER EVERYTHING THAT HAD HAPPENED ON ARUK DURING OUR BRIEF STAY...

...EVERYTHING WAS, FOR AN HOUR OR TWO, **PERFECT.**

WOW... **AMAZING.** YOU SAW THE TURTLE?

I DID. IS THIS **MORE** LIKE THE VACATION YOU WERE **PROMISED,** MS. CASTAGNA?

VERY **MUCH** SO, DR. DELAWARE.

I'M GOING BACK UNDER. YOU?

YEAH. GIVE ME A **MINUTE.**

ROBIN HADN'T SEEN WHAT I HAD: THE TWO SHARK BUTCHERS, SKIP AMALFI AND ANDERS HAYGOOD...

...STANDING CLOSE TO THE BLANKET WE'D SPREAD.

SOMEHOW, THEM BEING THERE MADE ME **UNCOMFORTABLE.** ENOUGH THAT I WANTED TO MAKE MY PRESENCE KNOWN.

BIG CRAB.

STONER. GOOD EATING.

CAN I GIVE YOU A COUPLE OF LEGS, SIR?

NO, THANKS.

GUESS WE HAVEN'T REALLY MET. ANDERS **HAYGOOD**. THIS IS SKIP AMALFI. SAW YOU AT THE **DOCKS** WHEN YOU ARRIVED.

AND THE AIRSTRIP.

HOW LONG YOU HERE FOR, DOC?

COUPLE OF MONTHS.

ISLAND'S **NICE**, RIGHT?

YOU THINK **RICH** PEOPLE WOULD **DIG** IT?

I GUESS **ANY-ONE** WHO LIKES SWIMMING AND RELAXING WOULD.

FUCKING **RIGHT**, MAN. ME AND MY BUDDY HAY WANNA BUILD A RESORT.

GRASS HUTS, LIKE CLUB MED. **CLASSY**. JUST NEED SOME INVESTORS.

SKIP, THE DOC DOESN'T WANT—

SHUT THE **FUCK** UP, MAN. I'M TALKING **BUSINESS** HERE. HE CAN—

GENTLEMEN...

GOT A NICE STONER THERE, HAY.

MUST BE SIX, SEVEN POUNDS OF MEAT.

DOCTOR DELAWARE, I **PRESUME.** **DENNIS** LAURENT, ARUK'S CHIEF OF POLICE.

NICE TO MEET YOU.

I SEE YOU'VE BEEN IN THE WATER, DOC. **NICE?**

... PERFECT.

ALWAYS IS. HAVE A NICE DAY, GENTLEMEN.

SKIP AMALFI AND ANDERS HAYGOOD. TOO MUCH FREE TIME AND ONLY **ONE** IQ BETWEEN THE TWO OF THEM.

THEY GIVE YOU ANY **TROUBLE?**

NO, NO TROUBLE.

SKIP HIT ON YOU FOR HIS **RESORT** SCHEME, RIGHT?

CAN'T YOU JUST **SEE** HIM GREETING BOAT-LOADS OF TOURISTS? "HEY, WELCOME TO **FUCKIN'** ARUK, MAN."

CHAMBER OF COMMERCE SHOULD HIRE HIM.

YEAH. IF WE **HAD** ONE. HELLO, MS. CASTAGNA. DENNIS LAURENT.

HOW WAS THE WATER?

WARM. NICE TO MEET YOU.

LIKEWISE. SORRY I DIDN'T FIND TIME TO INTRODUCE MYSELF EARLIER.

WE DON'T GET MANY **DEATHS** ON ARUK. WE'VE ALL BEEN BUSY.

NAVY JUST CALLED. THE PLANE WENT DOWN ON BASE PROPERTY. TOLD ME THEY'LL BE SHIPPING THE REMAINS BACK TO THE STATES.

BILLING MRS. PICKER LATER.

YOU'RE **KIDDING.** THAT'S **DESPICABLE.**

YUP. HOW'S MRS. PICKER DOING?

SHE LOOKED PRETTY **EXHAUSTED** THIS MORNING.

YEAH. I NEED TO TELL HER ABOUT TRANSPORTING THE BODY.

BETTER LEAVE **OUT** THE PART ABOUT THE **BILL** FOR NOW.

CAPTAIN EWING IS BEING A PAIN IN THE **ASS**, BUT IT'S NOT **HIS** FAULT THE BASE HAS NO MORTUARY.

NO SUPPLY BOAT FOR TEN DAYS. BODY'S GOING TO GET PRETTY **RIPE**.

SORRY.

EWING'S A PIECE OF WORK. MAYBE HE'S BITTER 'CAUSE HE GOT EXILED HERE AFTER THAT **SHIPJACK** SCANDAL.

ANYWAY, I'D BETTER GET GOING. AGAIN, NICE TO MEET **BOTH** OF YOU.

DO YOU KNOW IF DOCTOR **BILL'S** AT THE HOUSE?

YOU, TOO. NOT SURE ABOUT BILL. HE WAS THERE BEFORE LUNCH.

ALWAYS MOVING, MOVING, MOVING. NEVER MET A MAN **QUITE** LIKE HIM.

ANYWAY, IF YOU SEE HIM, TELL HIM HI. **PAM**, TOO.

WE DID SEE BILL WHEN WE GOT BACK TO THE HOUSE. HE TOLD ME **MILO** HAD CALLED.

HE SEEMED TO KNOW ALL ABOUT THE FAIR DETECTIVE STURGIS. HOW MUCH **RESEARCH** HAD BILL DONE ON ME? ON **US**?

MILO HAD A FEW QUESTIONS ABOUT DEALING WITH THE CONTRACTOR WHO WAS RE-BUILDING OUR HOUSE.

THEN HE ASKED ABOUT ARUK.

I HATE TO RISK **RAISING** YOUR CYNICISM QUOTIENT EVEN HIGHER. EVEN **EDEN** HAS ITS PROBLEMS.

I TOLD HIM ABOUT ANNEMARIE VALDOS'S **MURDER**.

CANNIBALISM?

CHRIST, AMIGO, YOU GO TO PARADISE AND **OUTDO** ME IN THE GROSSNESS DEPARTMENT?

TELL ME, IS THERE A GUY **STOMPING** AROUND THE ESTATE WITH A BAD HAIRCUT AND BOLTS IN HIS NECK?

DOES **ROBIN** KNOW ABOUT ALL THIS?

NOT ALL. DON'T WANT TO MAKE TOO BIG A DEAL OUT OF IT. OTHER THAN **THAT**, THERE'S BEEN NO SERIOUS CRIME HERE FOR YEARS.

"RIGHT...SO, ASIDE FROM THAT, MRS. LINCOLN, HOW WAS THE PLAY?"

BACK IN MY NEW OFFICE, I TACKLED ANOTHER BOX OF MEDICAL FILES.

MOSTLY *ROUTINE*; THE ONLY PSYCHOLOGICAL CONNECTIONS WERE STRESS REACTIONS TO PHYSICAL ILLNESSES.

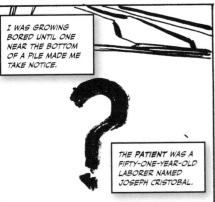

I WAS GROWING BORED UNTIL ONE NEAR THE BOTTOM OF A PILE MADE ME TAKE NOTICE.

THE *PATIENT* WAS A FIFTY-ONE-YEAR-OLD LABORER NAMED JOSEPH CRISTOBAL.

NO HISTORY OF MENTAL DISORDER, UNTIL HE BEGAN TO EXPERIENCE VISUAL *HALLUCINATIONS* AND SYMPTOMS OF *PARANOIA*.

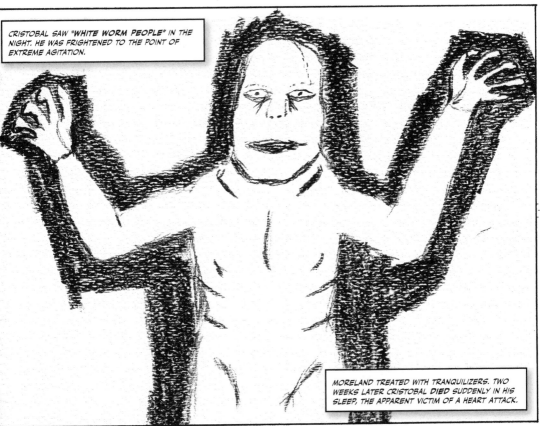

CRISTOBAL SAW *"WHITE WORM PEOPLE"* IN THE NIGHT. HE WAS FRIGHTENED TO THE POINT OF EXTREME AGITATION.

MORELAND TREATED WITH TRANQUILIZERS. TWO WEEKS LATER CRISTOBAL *DIED* SUDDENLY IN HIS SLEEP, THE APPARENT VICTIM OF A HEART ATTACK.

A NOTATION GOT MY ATTENTION. LIKE THE QUESTION MARK ON THE FILE FOLDER, IN **RED**, AND IN BILL'S HANDWRITING.

"A. *TUTALO.*" THAT LED ME ON A *SEARCH.* IT WASN'T THE NAME OF ANY BACTERIUM OR VIRUS IN THE MEDICAL DICTIONARY BILL HAD PROVIDED.

NATURAL HISTORY, ARCHAEOLOGY, MATHEMATICS, MYTHOLOGY, HISTORY, CHEMISTRY, PHYSICS, EVEN A COLLECTION OF ANTIQUE TRAVELOGUES. ONE COMPLETE CASE DEVOTED TO INSECTS.

NO ANSWER. I THOUGHT OF THE CAT-WOMAN. MORELAND'S TELLING ME ABOUT THE CASE MOMENTS AFTER WE'D MET.

NOW **ANOTHER** CASE OF SPONTANEOUS DEATH. AN EMERGING *PATTERN?*

HOW MUCH WAS DR. BILL *REALLY* TELLING ME?

I NEEDED SOME **AIR**. SOME TIME TO **THINK**. THE ROSE GARDENS WERE BEAUTIFUL AND FRAGRANT.

THE SMELL OF FRESH-CUT GRASS FROM THE LAWNS BROUGHT TO MIND CHILDHOOD SUNDAYS.

THE GREENHOUSES WERE KEPT SPOTLESS. EVERY PANE WASHED PERFECTLY CLEAR.

I KEPT WALKING.

THROUGH ALL OF BILL'S **PERFECTION**...

...TO THE **EDGE** OF THE ESTATE.

BARB WIRE ALONG THE TOP OF THE HIGH, CONCRETE WALL. **ALMOST** COVERED BY SWEET HONEYSUCKLE AND WISTERIA.

ALMOST...BUT THE ROUGH **EDGES** STILL SHOWED THROUGH.

ON THE OTHER SIDE, THE BANYAN TOPS FORMED A GREEN-GRAY AWNING, AERIAL ROOTS SHOOTING THROUGH THE CANOPY LIKE THE **TENTACLES** OF A BEAST IN PAIN.

FROM WHAT I COULD SEE, THE TREE TRUNKS BELOW WERE STOUT AND KINKED CRUELLY, WHIPSAWING IN A STRUGGLE FOR SPACE.

FOR A SECOND, THE ENTIRE FOREST SEEMED TO BE **MOVING**...TUMBLING DOWN ON ME...

...AND I FELT MYSELF LOSING BALANCE.

I FOUND THE WALL BEFORE I WENT DOWN. *BRACED* MYSELF WITH BOTH HANDS.

TRIED NOT TO LOOK UP.

ROBIN HAD WALKED THE EDGE OF THE ESTATE. SHE'D MENTIONED A SUBTLE *COOLNESS* DRIFTING OVER THE WALLS.

ALL I FELT WAS AN INTERNAL *CHILL.*

PROBABLY LOW BLOOD SUGAR. I HADN'T EATEN SINCE BREAKFAST.

I'D GRAB AN ORANGE FROM THE ORCHARD ON MY WAY BACK INTO THE HOUSE.

I GATHERED MYSELF AND WALKED *BACK.*

BACK TO MORELAND'S *PERFECT* LITTLE KINGDOM.

THE FOLLOWING NIGHT, ROBIN AND I MADE OUR BEST GUESSES AT "CASUAL FORMAL" AND HEADED TO THE HELICOPTER PICK-UP WITH BILL AND PAM.

FROM THERE, WE WOULD MAKE THE SHORT TRIP VIA HELICOPTER TO STANTON NAVAL BASE.

AS WE WAITED FOR OUR RIDE, TOM CREEDMAN APPEARED, ALSO INVITED. I COULD FEEL MORELAND TENSE UP. BUT HE FORCED OUT A SINGLE SYLLABLE GREETING.

TOM.

'EVENING, ALL. PRETTY NIFTY...PERSONAL AERIAL ESCORT AND ALL.

HOW GOES THE BOOK, TOM?

IT GOES. SLOW AND STEADY AND ALL THAT.

IT'LL BE—

I COULD FEEL BILL'S RELIEF WHEN THE HELICOPTER'S ENGINES MADE FURTHER CHATTER FROM CREEDMAN IMPOSSIBLE.

THE HELICOPTER NEVER FULLY LANDED. WE MADE OUR WAY UP A ROPE LADDER AND INTO THE CABIN.

THE SOUND OF THE TWIN ENGINES WAS **DEAFENING**.

AS WE FOLLOWED THE COASTLINE TO THE EAST SIDE OF THE BLADE-SHAPED ISLAND, THE DIFFERENCE IN THE TOPOGRAPHY WAS **STRIKING**.

THE **WEST** SIDE OF THE MOUNTAINS WAS THICK AND DARK WITH BANYANS. ON THE **EAST**, EVERYTHING TURNED GRAY. DEAD.

THE BASE WAS AS SAD AND DECREPIT FROM THE GROUND AS IT WAS FROM THE AIR. WE WERE HIT BY A BLAST OF HUMID AIR, STALE AND CHEMICALLY TAINTED.

THE WINDWARD SIDE OF THE ISLAND. NOTHING GROWS HERE.

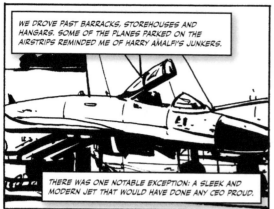

WE DROVE PAST BARRACKS, STOREHOUSES AND HANGARS. SOME OF THE PLANES PARKED ON THE AIRSTRIPS REMINDED ME OF HARRY AMALFI'S JUNKERS.

THERE WAS ONE NOTABLE EXCEPTION: A SLEEK AND MODERN JET THAT WOULD HAVE DONE ANY CEO PROUD.

PAST THE FENCE MARKING THE EDGE OF THE BASE, I COULD SEE THE BANYANS WHERE LYMAN PICKER MUST HAVE GONE DOWN.

THE BASE HAD TO BE RUN BY A SKELETON CREW. WE ONLY SAW A HANDFUL AS WE DROVE THROUGH.

WE WERE LED INTO A MEETING ROOM AND OFFERED DRINKS. THE MESS HALL WAS NEARBY. THE PLACE SMELLED OF CANNED VEGETABLE SOUP AND MELTED CHEESE.

GOOD MARTINI. NICE AND **DRY**. WHY CAN'T WE GET ANYTHING LIKE THIS IN THE VILLAGE, BILL?

LUCKY IF I CAN GET SWILL IMPORTED FROM MALAYSIA.

PITY.

HOW LONG DID YOU LIVE HERE WITH MOM?

TWO YEARS. TWO **LONG** YEARS.

AFTER TEN MINUTES, TWO MEN ENTERED. ONE OF THEM HAD TO BE SENATOR HOFFMAN. AT LEAST, HE LOOKED LIKE HOLLYWOOD'S *IDEA* OF A SENATOR.

BILL!

SENATOR.

OH, JESUS! CUT THE CRAP! HOW ARE YOU, MAN?

INTRODUCTIONS ALL AROUND. HOFFMAN WAS GOOD AT IT, PULLING EACH OF US IN FOR A SENTENCE OR TWO AND A FEW SECONDS OF SINCERE EYE CONTACT.

HIS STORY WAS A GOOD ONE, ACCORDING TO WHAT LITTLE I'D READ: BORN TO A YOUNG WIDOW IN A STRUGGLING OREGON LOGGING CAMP. A KOREAN WAR HERO AND SUCCESSFUL BUSINESSMAN BEFORE WINNING HIS FIRST SENATE RACE AT FORTY-THREE.

HIS DOCTRINE WAS THE AVOIDANCE OF EXTREMES; SOMEONE DUBBED HIM MR. MIDDLE-OF-THE-ROAD AND IT STUCK. TRUE BELIEVERS ON BOTH ENDS TRIED TO USE IT AGAINST HIM.

THE VOTERS IGNORED THEM. HOFFMAN WAS WELL INTO HIS THIRD TERM.

HOFFMAN INTRODUCED CAPTAIN EWING, WHO BARELY MANAGED NOT TO LOOK ANNOYED AT THE INTRUSION.

LET'S ALL GET SETTLED, SHALL WE?

SO GOOD TO SEE YOU, BILL. BEEN KEEPING UP WITH THE BRIDGE?

NO. HAVEN'T PLAYED AT ALL SINCE YOU LEFT, NICHOLAS.

DAD'S BEEN WRITING YOU LETTERS, SENATOR. DID YOU RECEIVE THEM?

I DID **INDEED**. TWO LETTERS, RIGHT, BILL? OR DID YOU SEND SOME THAT DIDN'T MAKE IT TO ME?

JUST TWO.

ARE YOU HERE TO **ASSESS** THE BASE, NICHOLAS? ARE YOU PLANNING ON **CLOSING** IT DOWN?

NOT AT THE DECISION STAGE YET. I CAN'T ELIMINATE ANY POSSIBILITIES, BILL.

IF THE BASE CLOSES, WHAT WILL HAPPEN TO **ARUK**?

YOU'RE PROBABLY IN A BETTER POSITION TO SAY, DON'T YOU THINK?

YES. I PROBABLY AM.

SECURITY.

ELVIN?

I WROTE ABOUT THE **BLOCKADE** OF THE SOUTH BEACH ROAD. DID CAPTAIN EWING GIVE YOU HIS REASON FOR IT?

SOMETIMES THINGS **CHANGE**, BILL.

SOMETIMES THEY **SHOULDN'T**, NICK.

SOMETIMES, UNDER THE GUISE OF HELPING PEOPLE WE DO **TERRIBLE** THINGS.

THE BLOCKADE WAS ECONOMIC OPPRESSION, PURE AND SIMPLE. IT IS **STRANGLING** THIS ISLAND.

EWING OFFERED EXCUSES THROUGH CLENCHED TEETH. "LOCAL UNREST" FOLLOWING AN INCIDENT. SOMETHING ABOUT THE PROPER AUTHORIZATION HAVING BEEN OBTAINED.

THERE WAS A MURDER. A GIRL RAPED AND CUT UP. THE LOCALS THOUGHT A SAILOR DID IT.

THINGS WERE GETTING **UGLY**.

GOBBLEDY-GOOK.

59

A FEW **KIDS** GOT OUT OF HAND.

IN RESPONSE, THE NAVY CHOKES OFF THE ISLAND'S ECONOMY.

WE'VE **EXPLOITED** THEM ALL THESE YEARS. IT'S IMMORAL TO SIMPLY YANK OUT THE RUG.

ANY EVIDENCE A SAILOR WAS RESPONSIBLE FOR THE GIRL'S MURDER, EWING?

NONE WHATSOEVER, SIR.

RUMORS. THE LOCALS GOT LIQUORED UP AND TRIED TO STORM THE BASE. THINGS MIGHT HAVE GOTTEN OUT OF HAND.

NONSENSE. IT'S THE SAME OLD PATTERN: ISLANDERS LIVING AT THE PLEASURE OF WESTERNERS ONLY TO BE ABANDONED.

IT'S A **BETRAYAL.** YET ANOTHER EXAMPLE OF ABUSING TRUST.

"A BETRAYAL."

BILL, YOU **KNOW** THAT ARUK HAS A SPECIAL PLACE IN MY HEART.

BUT THE WORLD'S **CHANGED.** SOME PEOPLE THINK WE NEED TO STOP ACTING LIKE UNIVERSAL NURSEMAIDS.

WE'RE TALKING ABOUT REAL **PEOPLE** HERE. A WAY OF LIFE!

WHOA, DOC. YOU MAKE IT SOUND LIKE EVERYTHING WAS JUST **PEACHY** BEFORE THE EUROPEANS CAME OVER AND SPOILED EVERYTHING.

MY RESEARCH TELLS ME THEY HAD **PLENTY** OF DISEASES IN THE PRIMITIVE WORLD.

LET'S GET REAL. WE'RE TALKING **PRIMITIVE** TRIBES. PAGAN RITUALS, NO INDOOR PLUMBING—

SO, IN ADDITION TO ALL YOUR **OTHER** TALENTS, ARE YOU ALSO A WASTE-DISPOSAL EXPERT?

THOSE "PRIMITIVES" GOT ALONG FINE UNTIL THE CIVILIZED **CONQUERORS** CAME ALONG...

...BRINGING FILTH, CHOLERA, TYPHOID. HAVE YOU EVER **SEEN** SOMEONE WITH CHOLERA, CREEDMAN?

HAVE YOU EVER HELD A CHILD IN YOUR ARMS AS SHE CONVULSES IN THE THROES OF DEADLY, EXPLOSIVE DIARRHEA?

NO.

I BOW, DOCTOR, TO YOUR SUPERIOR KNOWLEDGE OF DIARRHEA.

COME ON, BILL, LET'S YOU AND ME CATCH UP ON OLD TIMES.

NICE TO MEET YOU ALL.

EWING LEFT WITH BILL AND HOFFMAN. THE CAPTAIN COULDN'T WAIT TO GET OUT OF THERE. THE REST OF US ATE QUIETLY BEFORE BEING USHERED BACK TO THE HELICOPTER.

THE PRIVATE CHAT BETWEEN BILL AND HOFFMAN LASTED UNTIL WE WERE BOARDED. IT DIDN'T APPEAR TO BE SIMPLE, FRIENDLY BANTER.

AS BILL CLIMBED ABOARD, HE SAGGED WITH EXHAUSTION.

DAD, ARE YOU ALL—

I'M FINE, KITTEN. NOW...

"...LET'S GET THE **HELL** OUT OF HERE."

AFTER WE LANDED, CREEDMAN WALKED AWAY WITHOUT A WORD. NO ONE SPOKE DURING THE RIDE BACK TO THE ESTATE.

I THINK I'LL CATCH UP ON WORK. YOU ALL RELAX.

MAYBE I'LL GO INTO TOWN. I THOUGHT I MIGHT GO FOR A NIGHT SWIM.

OH?

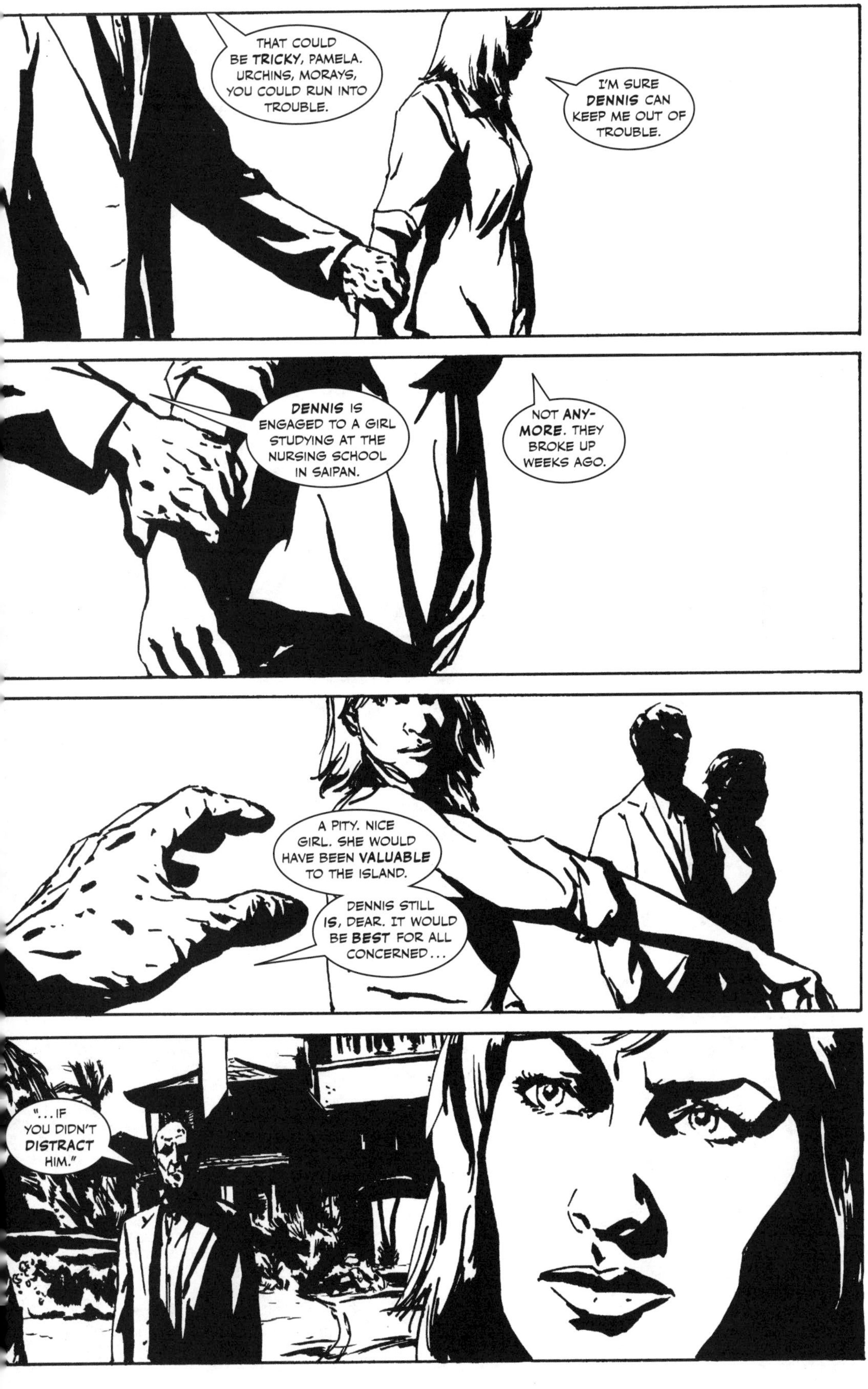
THAT COULD BE TRICKY, PAMELA. URCHINS, MORAYS, YOU COULD RUN INTO TROUBLE.
I'M SURE DENNIS CAN KEEP ME OUT OF TROUBLE.
DENNIS IS ENGAGED TO A GIRL STUDYING AT THE NURSING SCHOOL IN SAIPAN.
NOT ANY-MORE. THEY BROKE UP WEEKS AGO.
A PITY. NICE GIRL. SHE WOULD HAVE BEEN VALUABLE TO THE ISLAND.
DENNIS STILL IS, DEAR. IT WOULD BE BEST FOR ALL CONCERNED...
"...IF YOU DIDN'T DISTRACT HIM."

FUN EVENING.

THE WAY BILL JUST ACTED...SO HARSH.

YEAH. LOVES THE NATIVES BUT DOESN'T WANT THEM DATING HIS DAUGHTER?

IT ALMOST SOUNDED LIKE HE WAS SHIELDING DENNIS FROM HER.

IT DID. MAYBE SHE'S GOT AN UNFORTUNATE HISTORY WITH MEN.

THERE'S SOMETHING ABOUT HER THAT SETS UP A CLEAR BOUNDARY. I'VE SEEN IT IN PATIENTS: "I'VE BEEN WOUNDED. STAY AWAY."

THAT OBVIOUSLY DOESN'T APPLY TO DENNIS.

THE OLD MAN REALLY LOST IT. PERFECT CAPPER TO A CHARMING DINNER.

THAT BASE... IT FELT LIKE NIGHT OF THE UNIFORMED DEAD. AND HOFFMAN. JOE SLICK.

WHY DO I GET THE FEELING HOFFMAN'S SOLE PURPOSE FOR THE DINNER WAS THE TEN MINUTES HE AND MORELAND SPENT ALONE?

THE TENSION BETWEEN THEM...LIKE THEY HAVE SOME SECRET ISSUE THAT GOES WAY BACK.

AT ANY RATE, MORELAND DIDN'T GET WHAT HE WANTED FOR ARUK. WHATEVER THAT IS.

IF BILL IS AS RICH AS CREEDMAN SAYS, IT SEEMS LIKE HE COULD DO MORE TO REJUVENATE THE ISLAND ON HIS OWN.

MORE FREQUENT SHIPPING SCHEDULES, AT LEAST. BUT HE STAYS WALLED UP HERE LIKE SOME **LORD** WHILE THE ISLAND MOLDERS AROUND HIM.

THE ISLAND **ITSELF** IS SO ODD. SPLIT DOWN THE MIDDLE. ONE SIDE HAS GOOD WEATHER BUT NO HARBOR. THE HARBOR SIDE IS SO BARREN.

YEAH. NOTHING **FITS**. LIKE A GEOGRAPHIC JOKE. MAYBE EVERY-ONE GETS IT BUT MORELAND.

LOOKS LIKE I SIGNED ON WITH DR. QUIXOTE.

I'M GOING TO TAKE A QUICK BATH.

ONE PERK TO BEING HERE, AT LEAST. THE WRIST FEELS GOOD.

MIGHT EVEN TRY A LITTLE WORK TOMORROW.

ROBIN HAD BARELY STEPPED INTO THE BATHROOM WHEN SHE **SCREAMED**. UTTERLY TERRIFIED.

THREE OF THEM. NO, FOUR. *MORE!*

RACING BACK AND FORTH, LIGHT-PANICKED, ON THE WHITE FLOOR.

ARMORED SHELL AS LONG AS MY HAND. SIX BLACK LEGS. THE EYES, TOO DAMN SMART.

TRUE TO ITS NAME, IT *HISSED.*

HSS-ZZZZ

THEY *ALL* BEGAN HISSING.

SPEEDING TOWARD US.

I TUGGED ON ROBIN, HOPING TO GET OUT *BEFORE* THEY REACHED US.

OH GOD,
ALEX! OH GOD!

I WALKED IN
AND SOMETHING...
TOUCHED MY FOOT.

IT'S OKAY,
THEY CAN'T
GET OUT.

I WILL.

GET RID OF
THEM, HONEY.
PLEASE!

I CAN TAKE
THEM IN THEIR CAGES,
BUT GOD...THEY'RE
DISGUSTING!

JUST GET
THEM OUT OF
HERE, ALEX!

ALEX... SO *SORRY*. I DON'T SEE *HOW*...

DID YOU HAPPEN TO NOTICE WHAT *KIND* OF—

MADAGASCAR HISSING ROACHES.

OH... *GOOD*. THEY CAN'T *SERIOUSLY* HARM YOU.

CAREFUL! PLEASE...DON'T LET THEM OUT.

NO PROBLEM, DEAR.

I HOPE GLADYS WILL FORGIVE ME FOR RUINING HER TRAY OF BROWNIES.

HERE NOW... IT'S ALL RIGHT.

WE WAITED. SOUNDS CAME FROM INSIDE THE BATHROOM. MORELAND TALKING.

SOOTHINGLY.

YES, DEAR. EVERYTHING'S **FINE.**

YOU'RE **SURE** YOU GOT ALL OF THEM?

THUMPING FROM INSIDE THE BOX. AND HISSING.

NOT **REALLY,** BILL. HOW THE **HELL** DID THEY GET HERE IN THE FIRST PLACE?

MORE THUMPS AND HISSES. BILL'S TONE HIT ME AS PATRONIZING. I LOST IT.

I...DON'T KNOW. I'M SORRY. **DREADFULLY** SORRY. MY APOLOGIES TO BOTH OF YOU.

THEY'RE **DEFINITELY** FROM THE INSECTARIUM. ARUK HAS NO INDIG—

SO HOW'D THEY GET **OUT?**

I SUPPOSE... SOMEONE MUST HAVE...

I'M SO SORRY. I SUPPOSE I MUST HAVE LEFT THE LID OFF.

OUR DOOR WAS **LOCKED,** BILL.

YES. WELL, THEY'RE VERY GOOD AT COMPRESSING THEMSELVES.

AGAIN...I'M SO **TERRIBLY** SORRY. YOU HANDLED IT **PERFECTLY.** THANK YOU FOR NOT HARMING THEM.

SO...THAT'S IT FOR TONIGHT'S **ENTERTAINMENT**. I CERTAINLY **HOPE SO**, AT LEAST.

YOU GOING TO BE ABLE TO **SLEEP**?

HOPE SO. HOW ABOUT YOU?

MY HEART'S DOWN TO TWO HUNDRED BEATS A MINUTE. I THINK.

HMM... HARD TO TELL. I NEED TO COUNT FOR A **LONG** TIME.

SO, HOW LONG DO WE **STAY** IN BUG-LAND?

YOU WANT TO **LEAVE**?

PLANE CRASH, UNSOLVED MURDER, THE ZOMBIE BASE, SOME FAIRLY UNCONGENIAL PEOPLE. NOW **THIS**.

MAYBE I'M **NUTS** BUT I STILL LIKE IT HERE. AS WEIRD AS IT ALL IS, ARUK IS **UNIQUE**. EVEN BILL IS.

I'M JUST NOT SURE I WANT TO BE BACK IN L.A. NEXT WEEK, DEALING WITH ALL THE REAL WORLD **STRESSES** AND LOOKING BACK WITH REGRET. YOU KNOW?

HISSS...

OH! MAYBE I SHOULD HAVE **SPIKE** SLEEP IN THE BED AND PUT **YOU** IN THE CRATE!

A FEW SELF-CONSCIOUS JOKES ABOUT THE BUGS AND SHE WAS ASLEEP. I LIE AWAKE.

TRYING TO PICTURE THE ROACHES MAKING THAT LONG TRIP FROM THEIR HOME, THROUGH THE HOUSE, INTO OUR LOCKED ROOM AND BATHROOM. SEEMED LIKE A STRETCH. COULD SOMEONE HAVE PLACED THEM THERE? WHO, AND WHY?

BEN? GLADYS? CHERYL? JO PICKER HAD SOMEHOW SLEPT THROUGH THE WHOLE THING, JUST NEXT DOOR. ALL THE SCREAMING AND COMMOTION. WHAT POSSIBLE MOTIVE?

PARANOIA RUN AMOK.

I RELAXED MY MUSCLES CONSCIOUSLY AND DEEPENED MY BREATHING. SOON MY CHEST LOOSENED AND I FELT BETTER.

ABLE TO SMILE AT THE IMAGE OF MORELAND WITH HIS BALLED-UP BROWNIES AND SCHOOLBOY GUILT. MY BODY FELT HEAVY. READY TO SLEEP.

BUT IT TOOK A LONG TIME TO FALL UNDER.

I PITCHED THE UMBRELLA ON SOUTH BEACH AND REALIZED WE'D FORGOTTEN TO BRING DRINKS.

LEAVING ROBIN AND SPIKE ON THE SAND, I DROVE TO AUNTIE MAE'S TRADING POST.

THE PLACE WAS NO MORE CHEERY OR MAINTAINED ON THE INSIDE. STALLS FULL OF CLOTHING AND TOURIST KITSCH THAT NO ONE WANTED.

THE TV CAUGHT MY EYE...

SENATOR HOFFMAN. I ONLY CAUGHT PART OF HIS SPEECH.

SOMETHING ABOUT A VISION FOR A RENEWED, PROSPEROUS MICRONESIA FOR THE FUTURE.

CAN I HELP YOU?

SOMETHING TO DRINK, IF YOU'VE GOT IT. MAYBE SOMETHING TO READ, TOO. MAGAZINES?

I'VE GOT COKE AND SPRITE AND BEER. THINK I HAVE SOME MAGAZINES. YOU'RE THE DOCTOR STAYING WITH DR. BILL, RIGHT?

ALEX DELAWARE.

BETTY VAL... SORRY. AGUILAR. JUST GOT MARRIED.

CONGRATU-LATIONS.

THANKS... HE'S A **GREAT** MAN, DR. BILL. WHEN I WAS A KID I HAD A BAD WHOOPING COUGH AND HE CURED ME.

TWO COKES, TWO SPRITES, PLEASE.

SURE. OF COURSE, DR. BILL OWNS **THIS** PLACE. HE'S **REAL** GOOD ABOUT IT. DOESN'T CHARGE ANYONE RENT.

USED TO BE MORE BUSINESS, WHEN THE NAVY GUYS STILL CAME IN.

BOY, THESE ARE **REALLY** OLD. NO CHARGE, IF YOU WANT 'EM.

HALF-YEAR-OLD ISSUES OF READER'S DIGEST, TIME, NEWSWEEK, FORTUNE, AND SEVERAL COPIES OF A LARGE GLOSSY QUARTERLY ENTITLED ISLAND WORLD.

THOSE WERE EVEN OLDER. I FLIPPED THROUGH THEM AND A TITLE CAUGHT MY EYE.

THANKS. I'LL TAKE THESE.

I'M HAVING A **BABY.** DR. BILL'S GONNA DELIVER IT. IN SEVEN MONTHS.

THAT'S GREAT.

YEAH... WE'RE **EXCITED.** WE'LL PROBABLY MOVE AFTER, THOUGH. MY HUSBAND WORKS CONSTRUCTION. NO JOBS HERE.

AS I TURNED TO LEAVE, BETTY PLACED A HAND ON HER STILL-FLAT BELLY.

A SITCOM WAS STARTING ON THE TV. BETTY TURNED HER HEAD AND SMILED ALONG WITH THE LAUGH TRACK.

WHEN I GOT BACK TO THE BEACH, ROBIN'S SNORKEL WAS A TINY WHITE DUCK BOBBING NEAR THE OUTER EDGE OF THE REEF.

OUR BLANKETS WERE SPREAD, AND SPIKE WAS LEASHED TO THE UMBRELLA POST, *BARKING* FURIOUSLY.

IT TOOK MY BRAIN A SECOND TO PROCESS WHAT SKIP AMALFI WAS DOING...

PISSING ON THE SAND, VERY CLOSE TO OUR BLANKET AND SPIKE. AND *LAUGHING.*

THEY *TURNED* ... SAW ME COMING. I KEPT RUNNING FULL SPEED.

IS THAT GOING TO BE THE OFFICIAL WELCOME AT YOUR **"RESORT"**?

YEAH... *SURE.* LIVING NATURALLY.

BETTER WATCH THE ULTRAVIOLET RADIATION. IT CAN LEAD TO *IMPOTENCE.*

WHU...?

YOUR *HARD-ON.* WATCH THE UV ON YOUR TOOL OR YOU'LL BE HAULING LIMP WIENER.

FUCK YOU.

BOIL IT AND *SPOIL* IT.

HEY!

FUCK YOU IN THE *ASS,* MAN!

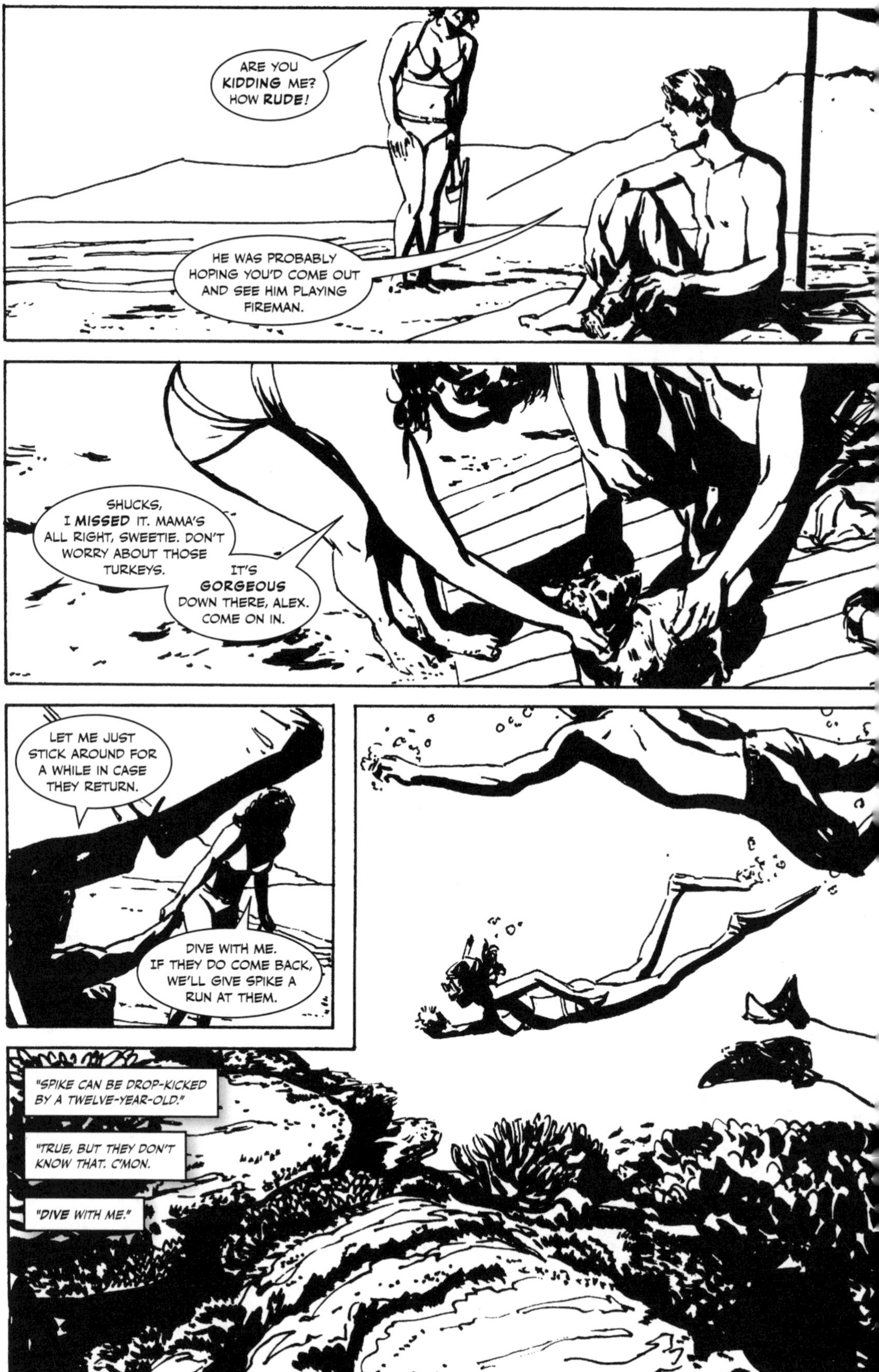

ARE YOU KIDDING ME? HOW RUDE!
HE WAS PROBABLY HOPING YOU'D COME OUT AND SEE HIM PLAYING FIREMAN.
SHUCKS, I MISSED IT. MAMA'S ALL RIGHT, SWEETIE. DON'T WORRY ABOUT THOSE TURKEYS.
IT'S GORGEOUS DOWN THERE, ALEX. COME ON IN.
LET ME JUST STICK AROUND FOR A WHILE IN CASE THEY RETURN.
DIVE WITH ME. IF THEY DO COME BACK, WE'LL GIVE SPIKE A RUN AT THEM.
"SPIKE CAN BE DROP-KICKED BY A TWELVE-YEAR-OLD."
"TRUE, BUT THEY DON'T KNOW THAT. C'MON.
"DIVE WITH ME."

THE DRINKS WERE WARM BY THE TIME WE EMERGED FROM THE WATER, BUT WE POURED THEM DOWN OUR THROATS.

I PICKED UP THE SPRING 1988 ISSUE OF ISLAND WORLD.

THE ARTICLE THAT HAD CAUGHT MY EYE WAS ON PAGE 113.

BIKINI: A HISTORY OF SHAME

THE STORY WAS IDENTICAL TO THE ONE MORELAND HAD TOLD ME: DEADLY, RADIOACTIVE DUST, DOCTORS DOLING OUT COMPENSATION. THE EXACT SAME STORY, DOWN TO THE AMOUNT OF MONEY PAID.

THE AUTHOR DID A THOROUGH JOB. A SIDEBAR LISTED THE DOCTORS INVOLVED IN THE PAYOUTS. NO **MENTION** OF MORELAND. IF HE'D BEEN INVOLVED, WHY WOULD BILL LIE ABOUT IT.

"GUILT IS A GREAT MOTIVATOR, ALEX."

DID BILL FEEL HIMSELF CULPABLE FOR THE BLAST? DID GUILT TRANSFORM HIM FROM A TRUST-FUND KID TO A WOULD-BE SCHWEITZER? MAYBE I WAS JUDGING HIM TOO HARSHLY, BUT THE LIES BOTHERED ME.

BACK AT THE ESTATE, WE ATE BROILED HALIBUT AND FRESH VEGETABLES. THEN I WALKED ROBIN AND SPIKE DOWN TO THE ORCHARD, AND HEADED FOR MY OFFICE.

MORELAND HAD LEFT ANOTHER FOLDED CARD ON MY DESK.

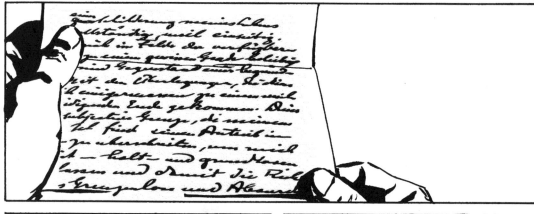

ANOTHER RIDDLE, AS IF BILL WERE PLAYING WITH ME. STRENUOUS IDLENESS? AND WHY HAD HE LIED ABOUT THE PAYOFFS?

TIME TO TALK.

BILL WASN'T THERE. AS I MOVED TOWARD THE LAB SOMETHING CAUGHT MY EYE ON HIS DESK. PRESS CLIPPINGS.

ABOUT ME.

ACCOUNTS OF TESTIMONY IN SEVERAL MURDER CASES. MY NAME HIGHLIGHTED. MILO'S, TOO. A NOTE ON ONE CLIPPING...

MY TESTIMONY DEBUNKING A PHONY INSANITY PLEA OF A MAN WHO HAD SAVAGED A DOZEN WOMEN. BILL WROTE "PERFECT!" IN THE MARGIN.

KRESSH

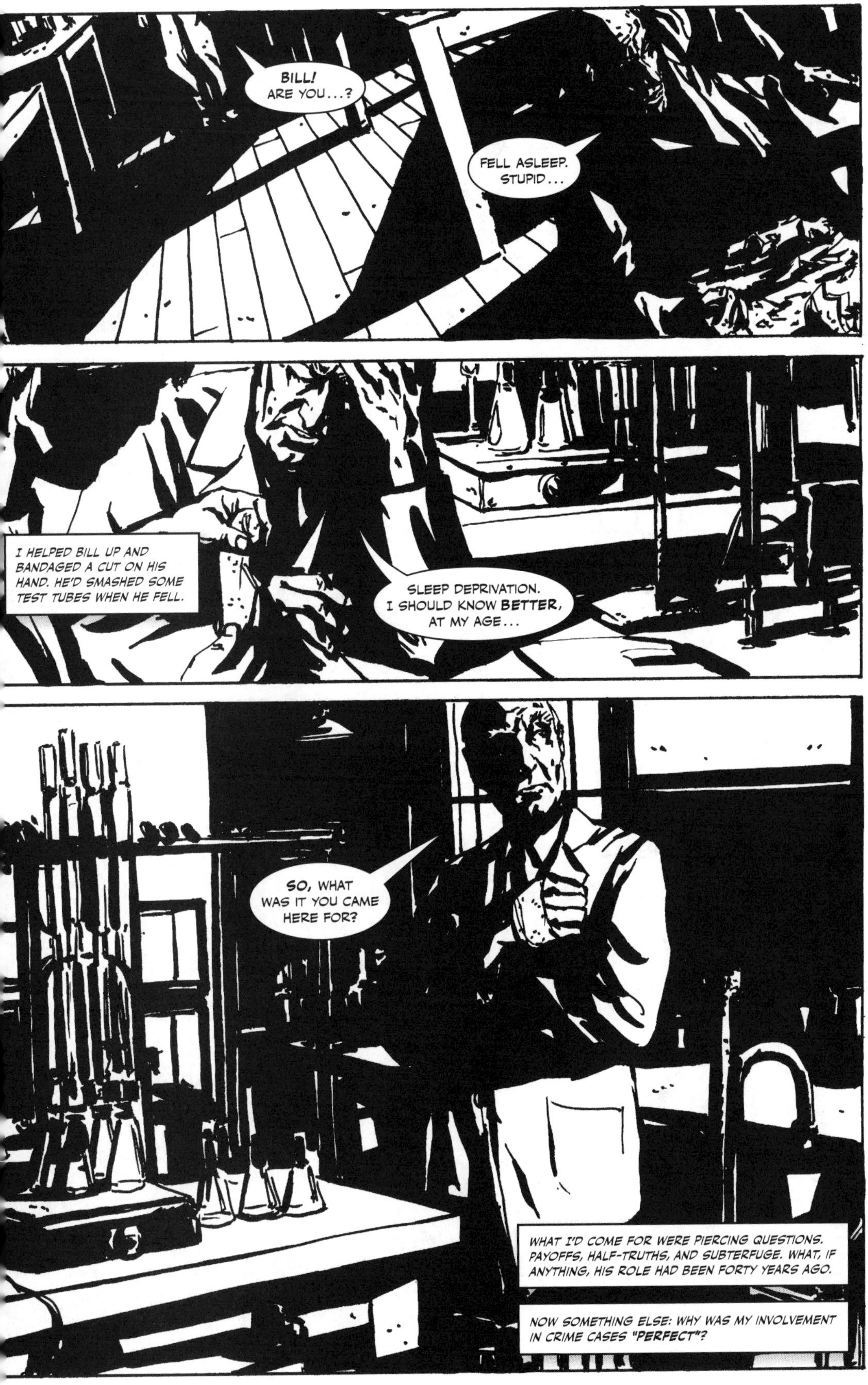
BILL! ARE YOU...?
FELL ASLEEP. STUPID...
I HELPED BILL UP AND BANDAGED A CUT ON HIS HAND. HE'D SMASHED SOME TEST TUBES WHEN HE FELL.
SLEEP DEPRIVATION. I SHOULD KNOW BETTER, AT MY AGE...
SO, WHAT WAS IT YOU CAME HERE FOR?
WHAT I'D COME FOR WERE PIERCING QUESTIONS. PAYOFFS, HALF-TRUTHS, AND SUBTERFUGE. WHAT, IF ANYTHING, HIS ROLE HAD BEEN FORTY YEARS AGO.
NOW SOMETHING ELSE: WHY WAS MY INVOLVEMENT IN CRIME CASES "PERFECT"?

I THOUGHT I MIGHT LOOK AT MORE RADIATION CASES. NEUROPSYCHOLOGICAL SEQUELAE OF RADIATION POISONING.

I DON'T THINK IT'S BEEN STUDIED BEFORE.

HE WAS SO TIRED. SO FRAIL. I PRESSED ON...GENTLY.

YES. UNFORTUNATELY, SAMUEL'S IS THE ONLY RADIATION CHART I TOOK WITH ME.

I'D ALMOST FORGOTTEN I HAD IT. SEEING IT AGAIN WAS A POTENT REMINDER.

OF WHAT?

THE TERRIBLE, TERRIBLE THINGS PEOPLE DO UNDER THE GUISE OF AUTHORITY.

SPEAKING OF AUTHORITY...

I TOLD HIM ABOUT HOFFMAN'S TV PERFORMANCE. HIS PLAN TO DEVELOP MICRONESIA.

"DEVELOP." HE'S MADE A FORTUNE LIKE THIS. DESTROYING NATURE TO BUILD SHOPPING MALLS AND CONDOMINIUMS.

HE TOLD ME ALL ABOUT THIS "DEVELOPMENT" LAST NIGHT. HIS PLAN TO LET ARUK DIE.

THE ISLAND ISN'T DEAD YET. AS YOU KNOW, A LOSS OF VIGOR DOESN'T IMPLY A **TERMINAL** STATE.

I STILL HAVE **HOPE. I ALWAYS** HAVE...

"...HOPE."

BILL TURNED BACK TO HIS WORK. I RETURNED TO MY OFFICE. WHY HADN'T I BEEN MORE FORTHRIGHT? THE FALL?

AN OLD MAN IN DECLINE? DECLINING ALONG WITH HIS ISLAND. BUT WHEN THE THOUGHT OF ARUK DYING HIT HIM...A SPARK. DEFIANT. ANGRY. A FLASH OF WHAT WE'D SEEN BETWEEN HIM AND PAM THE NIGHT BEFORE.

HOPE WAS FINE, BUT WHAT WAS BILL **DOING** TO SAVE ARUK? WHY DID HE SPEND HIS DAYS WITH INSECTS? **LORD** OF THE ROACHES. WHERE DID I FIT IN?

MY THEORY-SPINNING WAS CUT SHORT. PROBABLY JUST AS WELL.

ALEX...?

ROBIN... WHAT'S **WRONG?**

HERE... COME SIT DOWN.

WE TOOK ANOTHER WALK. TO THE NORTHEAST CORNER OF THE ESTATE. ACTUALLY, I JUST **FOLLOWED** SPIKE. HE KEPT PULLING ME THERE.

WE WENT THROUGH THICK PLANTINGS OF AVOCADO AND MANGO. SPIKE WAS REALLY HUFFING, PULLING ME AHEAD.

THEN I REALIZED WHY. SOMEONE WAS **CRYING** UP AHEAD.

IT WAS **PAM,** ALEX. LYING ON A BLANKET. PICNIC STUFF WITH HER. WEARING A SUNDRESS AND... OH BOY.

GOD, ALEX. IT WAS *MORTIFYING.* SHE WAS CLEARLY PLEASURING HERSELF, BUT *TEARS* ROLLED DOWN HER CHEEKS.

AND NOT TEARS OF ECSTASY. FOR SOME REASON, THE FEELINGS MADE HER *MISERABLE.*

THERE WAS NO SNEAKING AWAY DISCREETLY. *SPIKE* TOOK CARE OF THAT.

CAN YOU *IMAGINE?* A PLACE THIS SIZE, YOU'D *THINK* YOU COULD FIND SOME PRIVACY, AND LITTLE SHERLOCK BONES SNIFFS YOU OUT.

AFTER THE INITIAL SHOCK, SHE INVITED ME TO SIT DOWN. I WANTED TO BE *ANYWHERE* ELSE, BUT WHAT COULD I DO?

SHE PETTED SPIKE AND WE CHATTED FOR A WHILE. THEN...

...SHE *ERUPTED.*

A ROTTEN **MARRIAGE**. AN UGLY **DIVORCE**. HER HUSBAND **CHEATED** TIME AFTER TIME.

IT JUST POURED OUT OF HER. IT WAS ALMOST LIKE SHE WAS **HAPPY** I FOUND HER. NOW I SEE WHAT **YOUR** JOB IS LIKE.

BEFORE THE DIVORCE WAS FINAL, HER HUSBAND **DIED** IN AN ACCIDENT. A BARBELL FELL ON HIS **CHEST** DURING A WORKOUT.

OF COURSE, SHE FEELS **EXTREMELY** GUILTY, EVEN KNOWING THAT'S IRRATIONAL.

SHE DIDN'T ADDRESS THE FLAP OVER DENNIS, BUT YOU COULD SEE WHY BILL MIGHT BE OVER-PROTECTIVE.

YEAH. C'MERE. LOOKS LIKE YOU MISSED YOUR TRUE CALLING.

HARDLY. SHE JUST OPENED UP SO COMPLETELY.

NO SERPENTS. JUST **BUGS**.

GOD... THIS PLACE FEELS MORE LIKE EDEN AFTER THE FALL FROM GRACE WITH EACH DAY.

MAYBE WE SHOULD THINK ABOUT CUTTING OUR STAY **SHORT**, ROB.

WAIT. JUST... **HEAR** ME OUT. THERE ARE THINGS I HAVEN'T **TOLD** YOU.

I OPENED UP ON **EVERYTHING**: THE IDEA OF SOMEONE PLANTING THE ROACHES. BILL'S CLIP FILE AND THE MYSTERY OF WHY I WAS CHOSEN TO COME TO ARUK. ALL THE DECEPTIONS.

EVEN THE GRIM DETAILS OF THE MURDER. THE ORGAN THEFT, THE CANNIBALISM, **ALL** OF IT. I COULD SEE THE SHOCK ON HER FACE. AND THEN, THE **DISAPPOINTMENT** THAT I HAD HIDDEN IT FROM HER UNTIL NOW.

I'M **SORRY**, ROB. WE CAME HERE FOR A **VACATION**. WOULD HEARING ABOUT ALL THAT HAVE DONE YOU ANY GOOD?

BEING HERE... EVEN THE THING WITH PAM TODAY...IT'S BEEN A REAL **LEARNING** EXPERIENCE.

DON'T **WORRY**. I'M NOT PUTTING AWAY THE POWER TOOLS TO BECOME A THERAPIST.

TWO SHRINKS IN THE HOUSE WOULD BE A BIT MUCH. BUT HELPING PEOPLE **IS** GRATIFYING.

WELCOME TO ROBIN'S **EPIPHANY**. ALL THAT SAID, WE CAN LEAVE EARLY IF YOU'RE UN-COMFORTABLE.

NO, THERE'S NO **EMERGENCY**. I'M PROBABLY LETTING MY IMAGINATION GET OUT OF CONTROL, AS USUAL.

I **LIKE** YOUR IMAGINATION. THANKS FOR CALMING ME DOWN. HEY...YOU CAN BE **MY** THERAPIST.

NO WAY. **ETHICS**.

I WANT TO KEEP SLEEPING WITH YOU.

AFTER A LATE DINNER, WE RETIRED TO OUR ROOM. ALMOST IMMEDIATELY, WE WERE EMBRACING, **MERGING** HUNGRILY.

AFTERWARD, I SANK INTO A MOLASSES VAT OF DREAMLESS SLEEP, A WELCOME BRAIN-DEATH.

WE WERE AWAKENED BY THE SOUND OF RAPID POUNDING... FOOTSTEPS IN THE HALL. **LOTS** OF FOOTSTEPS. RUNNING.

THE SOUNDS OF **PANIC.**

WE SEEMED TO BE THE LAST ONES ON THE SCENE.

WE COULD HEAR BILL'S VOICE. ANGRY. INSISTENT. SHOUTING, "NO!"

IMPOSSIBLE, DENNIS! **INSANE!** IT JUST **CAN'T BE!**

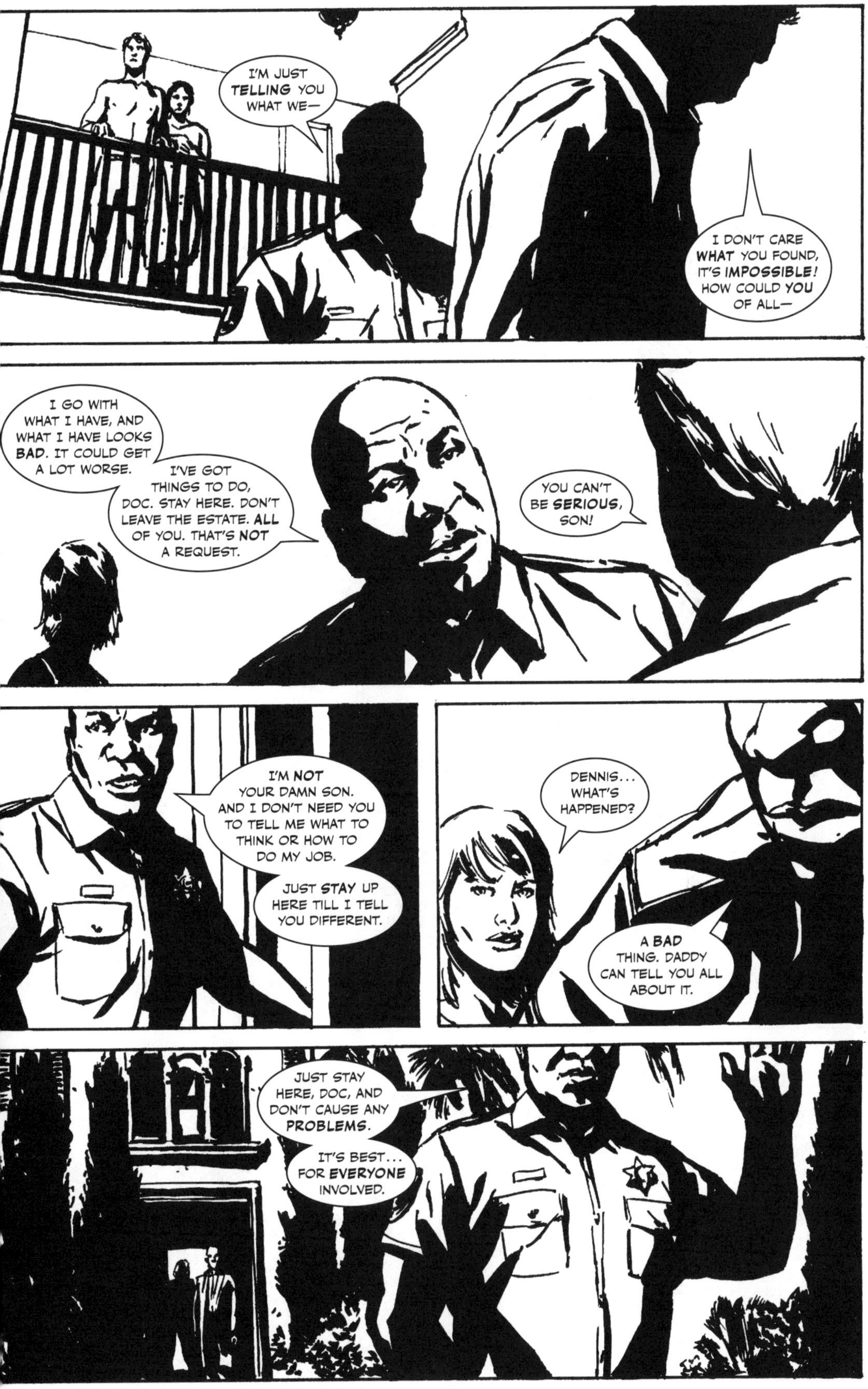

I'M JUST TELLING YOU WHAT WE—
I DON'T CARE WHAT YOU FOUND, IT'S IMPOSSIBLE! HOW COULD YOU OF ALL—
I GO WITH WHAT I HAVE, AND WHAT I HAVE LOOKS BAD. IT COULD GET A LOT WORSE.
I'VE GOT THINGS TO DO, DOC. STAY HERE. DON'T LEAVE THE ESTATE. ALL OF YOU. THAT'S NOT A REQUEST.
YOU CAN'T BE SERIOUS, SON!
I'M NOT YOUR DAMN SON. AND I DON'T NEED YOU TO TELL ME WHAT TO THINK OR HOW TO DO MY JOB.
JUST STAY UP HERE TILL I TELL YOU DIFFERENT.
DENNIS... WHAT'S HAPPENED?
A BAD THING. DADDY CAN TELL YOU ALL ABOUT IT.
JUST STAY HERE, DOC, AND DON'T CAUSE ANY PROBLEMS.
IT'S BEST... FOR EVERYONE INVOLVED.

BILL WAS A **WRECK**. PAM SUGGESTED WE ALL MOVE TO THE COOL BREEZE OF THE TERRACE. SHE FETCHED A GLASS OF WATER FOR HIM AND BRANDY FOR THE REST OF US.

THERE'S BEEN A CRIME. A **MURDER**.

A **TERRIBLE** MURDER. A GIRL NAMED BETTY AGUILAR.

MY **GOD**. THE TRADING POST GIRL. I JUST SPOKE TO HER **TODAY**. SHE WAS THREE MONTHS PREGNANT.

OH, NO.

I DELIVERED HER. I WAS GOING TO DELIVER HER BABY. I...I WAS OFFERING HER PRENATAL ADVICE.

BILL, WHY DOES DENNIS WANT YOU TO STAY HERE?

NOT JUST ME. **ALL** OF US. WE'RE ALL UNDER HOUSE ARREST, BECAUSE...

IT'S BEN. THEY THINK BEN DID IT.

INSANE. HOW COULD THEY **THINK** IT!

DENNIS CLAIMS BEN WAS THERE. AT THE SCENE.

"A MAN FROM THE VILLAGE WAS WALKING THROUGH VICTORY PARK, BY SOUTH BEACH. HE HEARD GROANS FROM THE BUSHES."

"HE FOUND...OH, DEAR **GOD**..."

"POOR BETTY. SHE WAS...CUT UP. **SAVAGELY.** A KNIFE STILL EMBEDDED IN HER THROAT."

"AND THERE WAS BEN, DRAPED OVER THE BODY. ASLEEP. **CONVENIENT, ISN'T IT?**"

"THE MAN WHO FOUND THE BODY CRIED OUT. SKIP AMALFI WAS NEARBY, FISHING. HE FANCIES HIMSELF SOMETHING OF A LEADER."

"SKIP HELD BEN DOWN, EVEN THOUGH HE WAS STILL UNCONSCIOUS. SUCH A **HERO.**"

THEY CLAIM HE WAS *DRUNK. RIDICULOUS.*

BOTH HIS PARENTS WERE DRINKERS. BEN STRUGGLED IN HIS TEEN YEARS, BUT HE'S BEEN CLEAN FOR *YEARS. I KNOW IT!*

BEN HAS *INCREDIBLE* STRENGTH OF CHARACTER! IT'S WHY I TOOK HIM IN. FINANCED HIS EDUCATION.

WHAT ARE YOU SAYING, BILL? SOMEONE POURED IT DOWN HIS THROAT?

I'M SAYING HE DIDN'T DO THIS. HE *COULDN'T* HAVE! WE'VE GOT TO *HELP* HIM!

WHAT ABOUT BETTY, BILL? SHE WAS *PREGNANT!* WHAT ABOUT HER UNBORN CHILD? HER HUSBAND?

OF COURSE. OF COURSE, THEY DESERVE SYMPATHY. I *ACHE* FOR THEM.

I STILL DON'T SEE WHY *WE'RE* ALL LOCKED UP HERE.

FOR OUR OWN *SAFETY,* SUPPOSEDLY. BEN WAS CLOSELY ASSOCIATED WITH THIS PLACE.

PEOPLE MAY TALK. TEMPERS MAY FLAIR, ACCORDING TO DENNIS.

ROBIN WENT TO BED, ALTHOUGH SHE DOUBTED SLEEP WOULD COME QUICKLY. I HAD A FEELING OUR HOST MIGHT STILL BE UP...

BILL?

ALEX. COULDN'T GET TO SLEEP, **EITHER**, I SEE.

I MIGHT HAVE, BUT I THOUGHT WE MIGHT AS WELL TALK. I NEVER FOLLOWED UP ABOUT A. TUTALO.

SURELY YOU CAN SEE WHY THAT WOULDN'T BE A PRIORITY RIGHT—

YES. VERY WELL. YOU WOULDN'T FIND MUCH IN MEDICAL BOOKS BECAUSE A. TUTALO IS A **FANTASY**.

NOT UNIQUE TO ARUK; WEREWOLVES, THE YETI, BIGFOOT, IT'S **ALL** THE SAME.

ARUK'S VERSION LIVE IN THE FOREST. PALE, SOFT AND HIDEOUS.

NO ONE BELIEVES IN THEM ANYMORE.

CRISTOBAL DID.

HARDLY BELIEF. JOSEPH HALLUCINATED. SUCH A STUBBORN MAN...

I **KNOW** IT'S BEEN A LONG NIGHT, BILL, BUT IF I'M GOING TO STAY HERE I NEED TO KNOW A FEW MORE THINGS.

WHAT ELSE TROUBLES YOU, SON?

I'D HAD ENOUGH OF BEING KEPT IN THE DARK, SO I PRESSED. I TOLD HIM HOW CUTOFF FROM THE REST OF THE WORLD ARUK SEEMED.

IF HE REALLY HAS HOPE, WHY NOT TAKE STEPS TO EASE THE ISOLATION? IMPROVE THE SHIPPING SCHEDULES. EVEN BUILD A NEW AIRSTRIP, INDEPENDENT OF THE NAVAL BASE.

I HATE TO **PRY**, BILL, BUT IF YOU HAVE AS MUCH OF A FORTUNE AS CREEDMAN SAYS—

CREEDMAN!

YOU CAN'T TRUST ANYTHING THAT MAN SAYS. *"JOURNALIST"* INDEED.

HE'S A CORPORATE **SHILL,** WRITING QUARTERLY RE-PORTS. HE LAST WORKED FOR **STASHER-LAYMAN.**

CONSTRUCTION CONTRACTORS. THEY CHEAT THEIR WAY TO WINNING GOVERNMENT BIDS AND BUILD GARBAGE.

CREEDMAN'S LAST REPORT MADE THEM LOOK LIKE **SAINTS.**

AS FOR MY **WEALTH**: I'M NOT TELLING YOU I'M POOR...

...BUT FAMILY FORTUNES RECEDE UNLESS SKILLFULLY TENDED TO. **BELIEVE** ME, I'M DOING ALL I CAN.

OKAY. SORRY FOR BRINGING IT UP.

NO APOLOGY NECESSARY. YOU'RE A **PASSIONATE** YOUNG MAN.

PASSIONATE BUT **FOCUSED**. RARE.

SO, DID DENNIS MENTION ANYTHING **ELSE** THAT LOOKS INCRIMINATING?

YES. THE WEAPONS USED WERE SURGICAL TOOLS. AN OLD SET...OF **MINE**.

MY **GOD**. DID BEN KNOW THE M.O. OF THE FIRST MURDER? IF BETTY WAS MADE TO LOOK LIKE A COPYCAT...

ONLY DENNIS AND I KNEW.

BUT, OF COURSE, BEN COULD HAVE ACCESSED YOUR FILES. WILL HE HAVE AN ATTORNEY?

DENNIS CALLED SAIPAN FOR A COURT-APPOINTED LAWYER. THE BOAT IS FIVE DAYS OUT.

93

FIVE DAYS. MY GOD. ARUK IS BEING STRANGLED. **ABANDONED.** I WON'T ABANDON BEN LIKE THAT.

BACK TO THE ISLAND FOR A MOMENT... DOES HOFFMAN HAVE A VESTED INTEREST IN ARUK'S DECLINE?

DOES **HE** HAVE TIES TO STASHER-LAYMAN, AS WELL? COULD **CREEDMAN** BE SOME KIND OF ADVANCE MAN?

STASHER-LAYMAN HAS BEEN DONATING TO NICHOLAS' CAMPAIGNS FOR YEARS.

I'VE WONDERED THE **SAME** THING ABOUT CREEDMAN.

BEN IS LIVING A **NIGHTMARE.** I THINK DENNIS WILL ALLOW YOU TO SEE HIM. WILL YOU GO?

JUST OFFER SOME PSYCHOLOGICAL SUPPORT. **PLEASE,** SON.

HE STARED AT HIS DEAD WIFE'S WATERCOLORS. PALMS OVER THE BEACH. WASHED-OUT HUES. NO PEOPLE. A **LONELINESS** SO INTENSE...

ALL RIGHT, BILL.

AS I LEFT BILL'S OFFICE I NOTED THAT THE TIME CHANGE MEANT MILO WOULD BE AT THE OFFICE.

STANLEY? IT'S LIVINGSTONE.

"WHAT'S UP? NO MORE CANNIBALS, I HOPE."

AS A MATTER OF FACT...

I FILLED HIM IN ON BETTY'S MURDER, ALONG WITH EVERYTHING ELSE THAT HAD BEEN ON MY MIND.

JESUS. I LOOKED AROUND ON THE COMPUTERS A BIT.

ONLY THING THAT POPPED IN RECENT YEARS WAS IN MARYLAND, NEAR D.C.

THOSE GUYS ARE STILL IN PRISON.

THINGS HAVE GOTTEN NUTS BUT SUCKING OUT A LADY'S BONE MARROW STILL MAKES PAROLE A TOUGH SELL.

THE MENTION OF D.C. CLICKED. I TOLD MILO ABOUT CREEDMAN AND STASHER-LAYMAN.

I'VE HEARD OF THEM. WHAT'RE THEY PLANNING TO BUILD OVER THERE?

NOT SURE. WOULD YOU MIND LOOKING UP BEN FOR ME?

JUST TO SEE IF THERE'S SOMETHING MORELAND DOESN'T KNOW... OR DIDN'T MENTION?

YEAH... CALL BACK ANYTIME. WE'RE NOT *GOING* ANY-WHERE. DENNIS LAURENT, THE POLICE CHIEF, HAS US ALL UNDER HOUSE ARREST.

"REALLY? NOT VERY FRIENDLY, OR *LEGAL*. WANT ME TO HAVE A COP-TO-COP CHAT WITH HIM?"

THANKS. NO... I THINK THAT MIGHT JUST MAKE MATTERS *WORSE*.

ALL RIGHT. I'LL SEE WHAT I CAN FIND.

YOU STAY *CAREFUL*, MAN. BUGS AND CANNIBALS. *ALMOST* AS BAD AS HOLLYWOOD BOULEVARD.

I FELT *RANCID* WHEN I GOT BACK TO THE ROOM. I SHOWERED. ROBIN WAS AWAKE WHEN I EMERGED.

I TOLD HER ABOUT MY TALKS WITH BILL AND MILO, AND DROPPED A *NEW* TIDBIT...I WANTED US TO BOOK THE NEXT BOAT OUT.

SHE DIDN'T ARGUE.

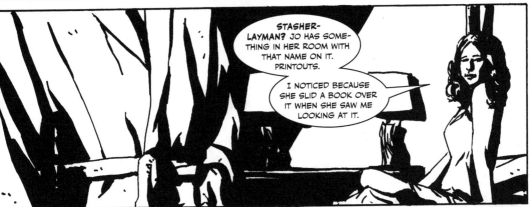

STASHER-LAYMAN? JO HAS SOMETHING IN HER ROOM WITH THAT NAME ON IT. PRINTOUTS.

I NOTICED BECAUSE SHE SLID A BOOK OVER IT WHEN SHE SAW ME LOOKING AT IT.

JO AND CREEDMAN. THEY COULD *BOTH* BE ADVANCE AGENTS. I'VE WONDERED ABOUT HER SINCE THE ROACHES.

I THOUGHT I WAS BEING PARANOID, BUT SHE WAS HERE ALONE THAT NIGHT. AND SOMEHOW *SLEPT* THROUGH ALL THE COMMOTION.

IF THIS COMPANY BUILDS THINGS, WHY *ARUK?* WHAT GOOD COULD THIS LAND DO THEM?

YOU SAID THEY BUILD CHEAP STUFF FOR GOVERNMENT BIDS. STUFF LIKE *PRISONS?*

THAT WOULD BE *PERFECT.* NO LOCALS TO PROTEST. WHAT BETTER PLACE TO DUMP FELONS?

IT WOULD BE POLITICALLY *BEAUTIFUL.* ENTER THE GOOD SENATOR.

STASHER- LAYMAN PAYS HOFFMAN OFF. HE **HAPPENS** TO KNOW OF A REMOTE ISLAND... HE BURIES IT ALL IN A BIG BILL.

PACIFIC RIM REVITALIZATION. WHO'D **NOTICE**, ASIDE FROM BILL?

THAT TALK THEY HAD. I WONDER IF HOFFMAN **PRESSURED** BILL. **THREATENED** HIM IN SOME WAY.

WITH **WHAT**?

I DON'T KNOW, BUT I HAVE THIS FEEL- ING THERE'S **SOMETHING** THERE THAT GOES WAY BACK.

BILL SAID, "GUILT IS A GREAT MOTIVATOR." LIKE HE'S TRYING TO **ATONE** FOR SOMETHING...

HE'S SUCH AN ENIGMA.

YOU KNOW, **DESPITE** ALL THAT'S HAPPENED, I HAVE NO REGRETS ABOUT COMING HERE.

ME, NEITHER. I'LL BOOK THE TRAVEL TO- MORROW. THEN I'LL FIND A WAY TO TELL BILL...

"ACTUALLY," HE SAID, "MAYBE YOU **SHOULD** COME DOWN TO TALK TO HIM. HE'S ACTING NUTS, AND I DON'T WANT TO BE ACCUSED OF NOT PROVIDING PROPER CARE, CREATE ANY TECHNICALITIES."

THAT WAS DENNIS'S ANSWER WHEN I CALLED HIM MID-MORNING TO ASK ABOUT SEEING BEN. HE PICKED ME UP, EMOTIONS HIDDEN BEHIND MIRRORED SHADES.

THERE WAS A **SHOTGUN** CLAMPED TO THE DASH OF HIS CAR.

WE DROVE BY A RESTLESS-LOOKING CROWD OUTSIDE SLIM'S BAR. I PICKED OUT SKIP AMALFI AND HIS DAD. THERE WAS A SIMILAR CROWD OUTSIDE THE MUNICIPAL CENTER.

THEY **PARTED** AS DENNIS WALKED IN, SHOTGUN IN HAND. I FOLLOWED IN HIS WAKE, LOOKING STRAIGHT AHEAD.

BEN HAD BEEN SILENT SINCE HE CAME TO. *MORE* THAN SILENT. HE WAS PULLING A COMPLETE STATUE ACT.

I WOULD BE ALLOWED TO TALK TO BEN, *ALONE*, FOR *ONE* HOUR. DENNIS WOULD HAVE DONE HIS PART. IF BEN WERE HELPED BY MY PRESENCE, SO BE IT.

TEN MINUTES, DR. DELAWARE...

DENNIS *ALSO* DROPPED A NEW BOMBSHELL ABOUT BEN'S PAST. THINGS WERE STACKING UP *NICELY* AGAINST HIM.

THE PLACE WAS HELLISH. *UNBEARABLY* HOT. THE SMELL WAS EVEN *WORSE*. IF BEN NOTICED EITHER, HE GAVE NO INDICATION.

"...NO MORE."

HELLO, BEN.

BILL SENT ME TO SEE IF THERE'S ANYTHING I CAN DO FOR YOU.

HIS ARM TENSED, RESISTING. NO CATATONIA.

NOT EXACTLY THE BEHAVIOR OF AN *INNOCENT* MAN, BEN.

WHAT ABOUT YOUR *FAMILY?* CLAIRE AND THE KIDS?

IF YOU BUTCHERED BETTY ON YOUR OWN, JUST ADMIT IT.

PEOPLE ARE *TALKING.* THEY SUSPECT **MORELAND** WAS INVOLVED.

IS THAT WHY YOU WON'T TALK? BECAUSE HE *WAS?*

MY BUTTON-PUSHING FINALLY GOT SOME *REACTION.* A SLIGHT FLINCH.

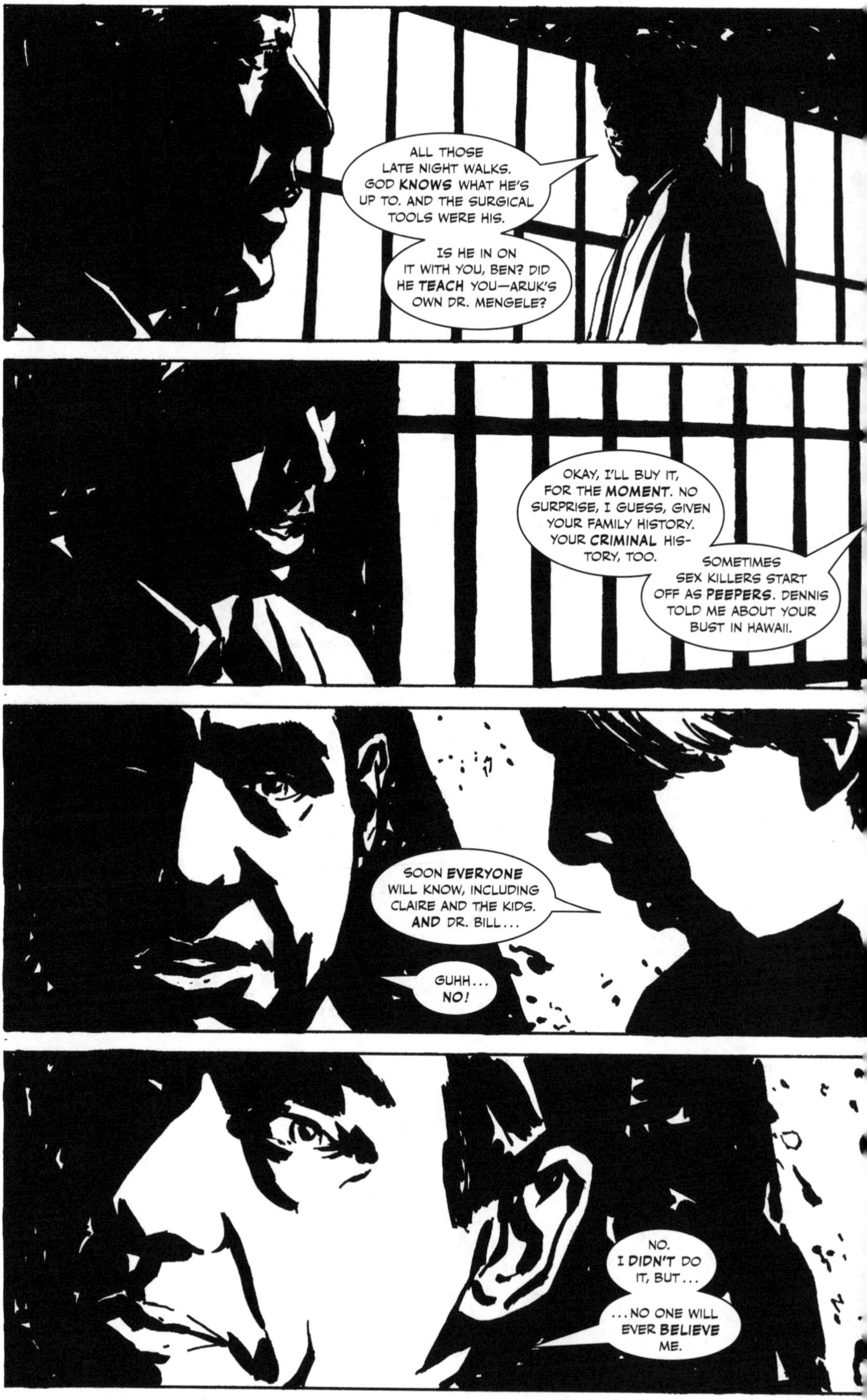
ALL THOSE LATE NIGHT WALKS. GOD KNOWS WHAT HE'S UP TO. AND THE SURGICAL TOOLS WERE HIS.
IS HE IN ON IT WITH YOU, BEN? DID HE TEACH YOU—ARUK'S OWN DR. MENGELE?
OKAY, I'LL BUY IT, FOR THE MOMENT. NO SURPRISE, I GUESS, GIVEN YOUR FAMILY HISTORY. YOUR CRIMINAL HIS-TORY, TOO.
SOMETIMES SEX KILLERS START OFF AS PEEPERS. DENNIS TOLD ME ABOUT YOUR BUST IN HAWAII.
SOON EVERYONE WILL KNOW, INCLUDING CLAIRE AND THE KIDS. AND DR. BILL...
GUHH... NO!
NO. I DIDN'T DO IT, BUT...
...NO ONE WILL EVER BELIEVE ME.

WHY WON'T ANYONE BELIEVE YOU, BEN?

YOU DON'T.

TELL ME WHY I SHOULD.

SOME KIND OF SELF-PRESERVATION FINALLY KICKED IN. BEN TALKED.

I DON'T **HAVE** AN ALIBI. I WASN'T DRINKING. THAT MUCH I DO KNOW.

"I GOT A CALL ABOUT A MEDICAL EMERGENCY AT THE PARK. I THOUGHT IT **MIGHT** HAVE BEEN THE GARDENER, CARL SLEET. I'M **NOT SURE.** THE MAN WAS PANICKED. TALKING SO FAST..."

"AT THE PARK, I SAW SOMEONE ON THE GROUND. I WENT TO THEM..."

"...AND SOMEONE **GRABBED** ME FROM BEHIND."

BEN SHOWED ME **HOW** HE'D BEEN GRABBED. SOMETHING LIKE A **POLICE** CHOKE HOLD.

BEN ALSO TALKED ABOUT THE PEEPING BUST IN HAWAII. HE FELL OFF THE WAGON FOR A NIGHT. RELIEVED HIMSELF IN THE BUSHES. GOT CAUGHT. IT WAS DUMB, BUT JUST THAT. HE'D BEEN **SOBER** EVER SINCE.

WITH EVERYTHING STACKED SO **NEATLY** AGAINST BEN, FINDING ALTERNATE SCENARIOS FOR HOW BETTY HAD ENDED UP DEAD WAS A DIFFICULT EXERCISE AT BEST. BUT...IF BEN WAS FABRICATING THIS STORY, HE WAS AN **AMAZING** PERFORMER.

THE DOOR TO THE CELLS OPENED UP AND DENNIS CAME TO GET ME. OUR TEN MINUTES WERE UP. BEN HAD JUST **ONE** MORE THING TO SAY...

PLEASE... TELL MY WIFE I'M SORRY. FOR **EVERYTHING.**

WELL, DR. BILL HAS BEEN **BUSY** TODAY. GOT A CALL FROM OAHU. HIGH-POWERED LAWYER ON THE WAY.

FLYING IN ON A PRIVATE JET IN A FEW DAYS.

MUST BE **NICE** TO BE RICH. C'MON... I'LL TAKE YOU BACK.

TIME FOR WIMBLEDON, TOM?

SURE. GONNA HAVE TEA WITH THE QUEEN AT MID-COURT. GOT A MINUTE TO TALK, DENNIS?

NOT **EVEN** HALF OF ONE. COME ON, DOCTOR.

SEE THE SUSPECT, DR. DELAWARE?

HOW 'BOUT COFFEE AT MY PLACE TO TALK ABOUT IT?

SURE.

I'M TAKING YOU **BACK.** FOR YOUR OWN SAFETY. **BESIDES,** YOU ARE CONFINED TO THE—

WHAT LAW GIVES YOU THE **RIGHT** TO RESTRICT MY MOVE-MENT?

MAYBE I SHOULD CALL BEN'S NEW LAWYER AND ASK **THEIR** OPINION.

FINE. YOU'RE ON YOUR OWN.

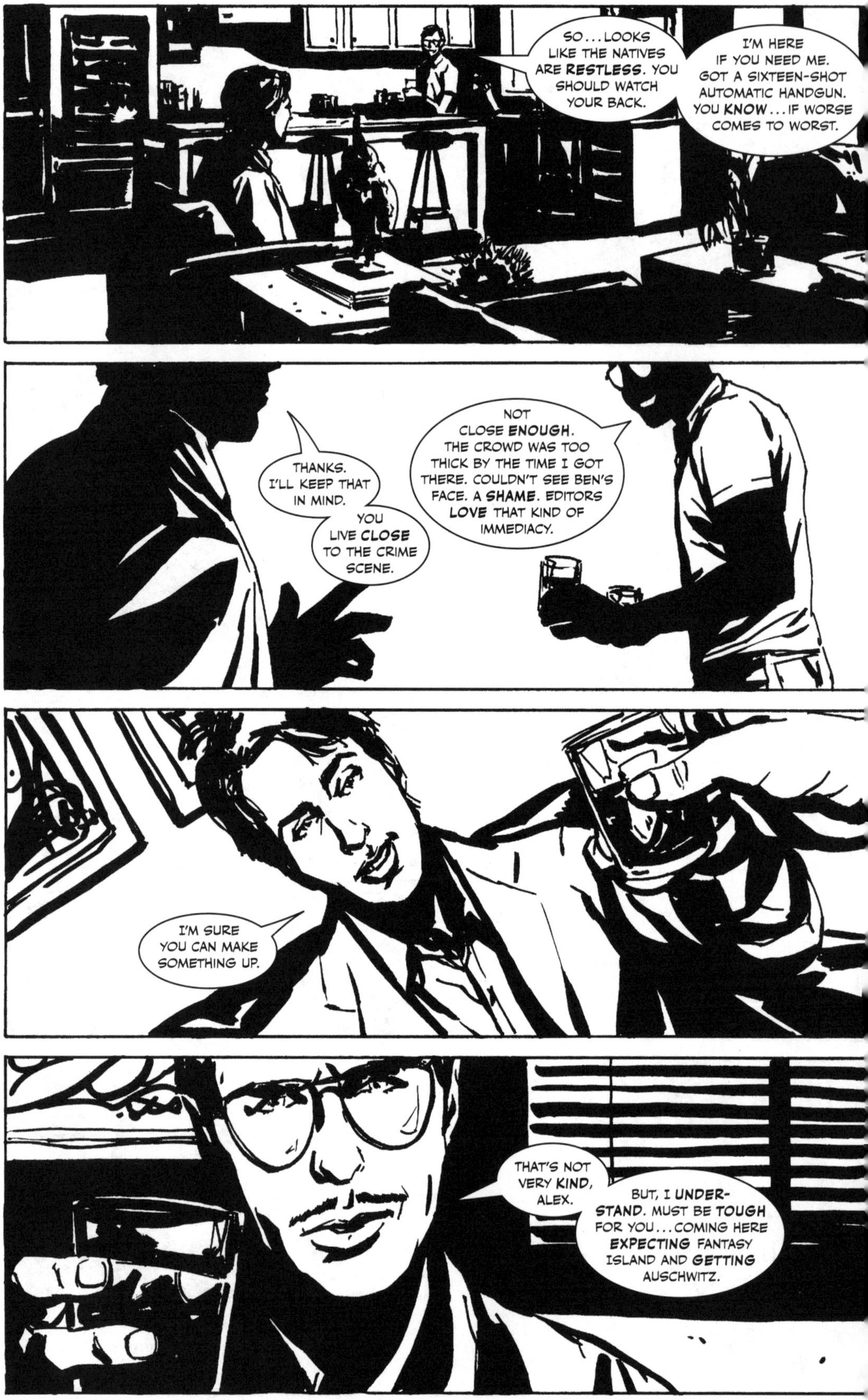
SO...LOOKS LIKE THE NATIVES ARE RESTLESS. YOU SHOULD WATCH YOUR BACK.
I'M HERE IF YOU NEED ME. GOT A SIXTEEN-SHOT AUTOMATIC HANDGUN. YOU KNOW...IF WORSE COMES TO WORST.
THANKS. I'LL KEEP THAT IN MIND.
YOU LIVE CLOSE TO THE CRIME SCENE.
NOT CLOSE ENOUGH. THE CROWD WAS TOO THICK BY THE TIME I GOT THERE. COULDN'T SEE BEN'S FACE. A SHAME. EDITORS LOVE THAT KIND OF IMMEDIACY.
I'M SURE YOU CAN MAKE SOMETHING UP.
THAT'S NOT VERY KIND, ALEX.
BUT, I UNDERSTAND. MUST BE TOUGH FOR YOU...COMING HERE EXPECTING FANTASY ISLAND AND GETTING AUSCHWITZ.

NICE PLACE. LOOKS LIKE YOU'VE **SETTLED** IN FOR THE LONG RUN.

I LIKE TO LIVE WELL.

SO...WHAT ABOUT YOU. PROBABLY CAN'T **WAIT** TO GET OUT OF THIS PLACE.

NO PLANS. WE'LL LEAVE... EVENTUALLY.

SO...ANY CHANCE **MORELAND** PUT BEN UP TO KILLING THOSE GIRLS?

WHY WOULD HE?

LET'S FACE IT, THE GUY'S **STRANGE**. THAT PLACE...THOSE **BUGS** OF HIS. AND WHAT THE HELL DOES HE **DO** ALL DAY IN THAT LAB?

WHAT THE **HELL** IS HE UP TO?

YOU'VE BEEN WORKING WITH HIM, ALEX. **C'MON**...

...WHAT'S HE **HIDING**?

107

I DON'T KNOW THAT HE'S HIDING ANYTHING.

I DO. I LIVED AT WEIRD CASTLE FOR AWHILE.

ALL THAT DO-GOODING AND HIS BEST BOY'S A SERIAL KILLER. PEOPLE ARE PISSED, ALEX. THEY'VE HAD ENOUGH OF MORELAND'S ACT.

IF YOU CARE ABOUT THAT PRETTY LADY AND THAT CUTE LITTLE POOCH, YOU'LL HEAD BACK TO LALA LAND PRONTO.

A WARNING, TOM?

JUST A WORD TO THE WISE. STRATEGIC ASSESSMENT BASED ON THE DATA AT HAND.

AND THAT SOUNDS KIND OF CORPORATE. ALMOST LIKE A QUARTERLY REPORT.

I'D BETTER BE GETTING BACK.

TOM TRIED TO HIDE A GUILTY EXPRESSION. HE FELL SHORT.

TOM GRACIOUSLY OFFERED A RIDE. CONVENIENTLY, HIS CAR WOULDN'T START. SOMETHING ABOUT A DEAD BATTERY.

JUST WON'T TURN OVER. I FEEL TERRIBLE.

SO SORRY. THANKS FOR THE CHAT.

HE DIDN'T SOUND A BIT SORRY.

I'D ACCEPTED CREEDMAN'S INVITATION TO CHECK HIM OUT. HE'D ASKED **ME** THERE FOR THE SAME REASON.

HIS PLACE WAS WELL-FURNISHED. HIS REACTION TO MY CRACK ABOUT QUARTERLY REPORTS TOLD ME STASHER-LAYMAN WAS PROBABLY FOOTING THE BILL.

I COULDN'T ASK **DENNIS** FOR A RIDE BACK TO THE ESTATE.

BEFORE I COULD COME UP WITH A VIABLE ALTERNATIVE, I HEARD **FOOTSTEPS** BEHIND ME.

NEAR SLIM'S I PICKED UP SOME SPEED AND CROSSED THE STREET. THE LOCALS KEPT UP.

I LOOKED BACK LONG ENOUGH TO SEE THAT ONE OF THEM WAS CARRYING A SHORT CLUB.

I **RAN.** SLIM'S WAS CLOSED, BUT SEVERAL BEER SWILLERS LOITERED NEAR THE PATIO.

I DOUBTED THEY WOULD PROVE ANY MORE **FRIENDLY** THAN THE KIDS BEHIND ME.

AS I GOT CLOSER, THEY FORMED A HUMAN WALL IN FRONT OF ME. SKIP AND ANDERS WERE AMONG THEM.

SKIP LOOKED FLUSHED. HIS LIPS WERE PURSED IN AN ATTEMPTED BELCH. ANDERS WAS AMUSED.

THE BOYS TO MY BACK **SHOUTED** SOMETHING. THE SLIM'S CROWD MOVED FORWARD.

CAUGHT IN THE MIDDLE.

IDIOTS!

MORE SHOUTS. LOUD MURMURING, AND THEN A VOICE CUT THROUGH EVERYTHING.

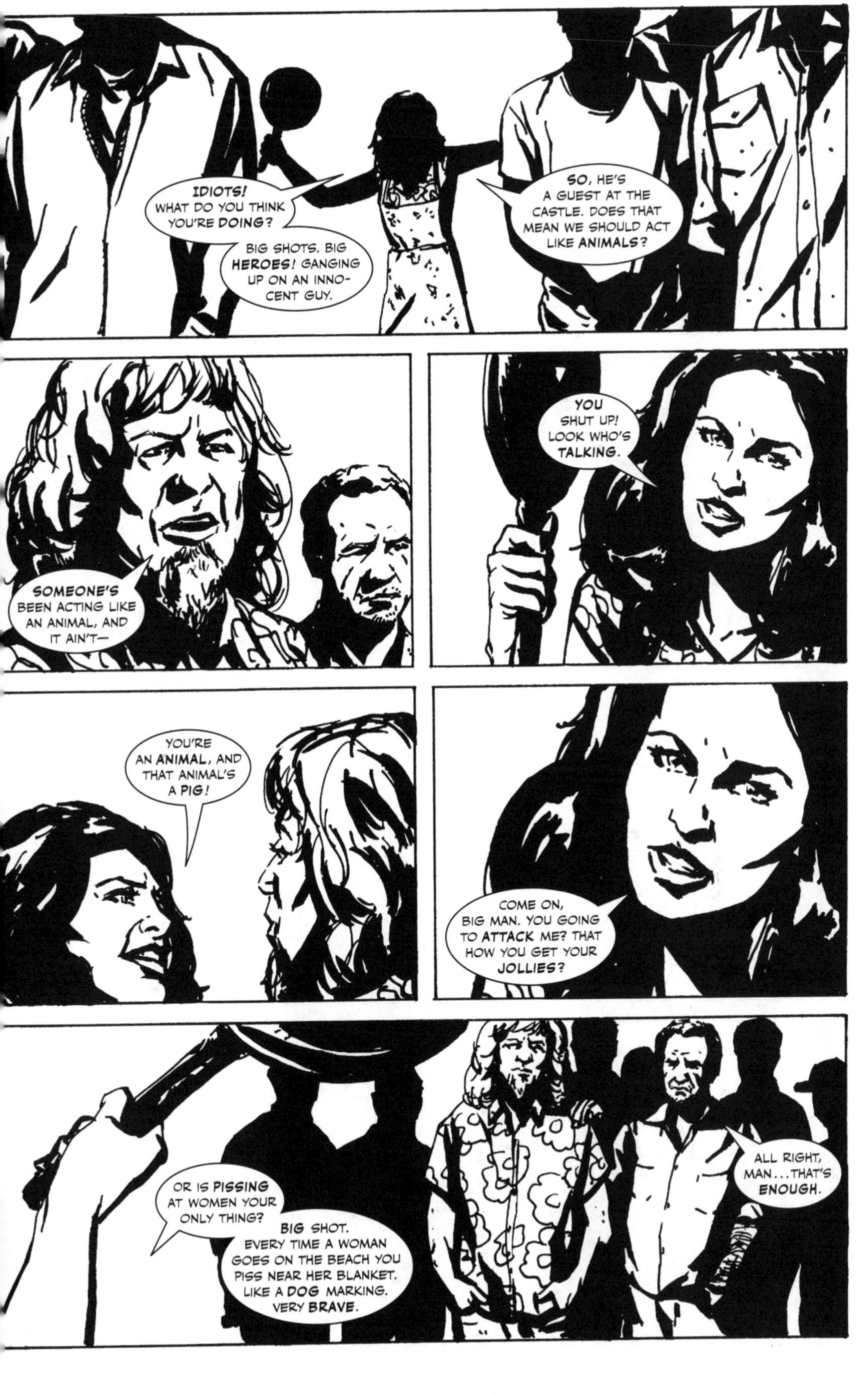
IDIOTS! WHAT DO YOU THINK YOU'RE DOING?
BIG SHOTS. BIG HEROES! GANGING UP ON AN INNO-CENT GUY.
SO, HE'S A GUEST AT THE CASTLE. DOES THAT MEAN WE SHOULD ACT LIKE ANIMALS?
SOMEONE'S BEEN ACTING LIKE AN ANIMAL, AND IT AIN'T—
YOU SHUT UP! LOOK WHO'S TALKING.
YOU'RE AN ANIMAL, AND THAT ANIMAL'S A PIG!
COME ON, BIG MAN. YOU GOING TO ATTACK ME? THAT HOW YOU GET YOUR JOLLIES?
OR IS PISSING AT WOMEN YOUR ONLY THING?
BIG SHOT. EVERY TIME A WOMAN GOES ON THE BEACH YOU PISS NEAR HER BLANKET. LIKE A DOG MARKING. VERY BRAVE.
ALL RIGHT, MAN...THAT'S ENOUGH.

GIVE ME **THAT**. YOU LIKE TO GET **TOUGH** WITH WOMEN, TOO?

YOU'RE ALL SO **TOUGH**. MAYBE SOME OF YOU HAD SOMETHING TO DO WITH BETTY!

BIG, TOUGH **MACHO** MEN! GANG UP ON A GUEST. WHAT'S HIS **CRIME**? **VISITING**? HOW DO YOU THINK **THAT** MAKES THE ISLAND LOOK?

YOU SHOULD BE **ASHAMED** OF YOURSELVES.

AND WHAT DID YOU THINK **YOU** WERE DOING? THIS IS NOT THE TIME TO PLAY TOURIST.

SO I **SEE**. THANK YOU.

COME ON, I'LL GET DENNIS TO DRIVE YOU.

I SAID **COME** ON. HE'LL GIVE YOU A RIDE.

HE ALREADY OFFERED. I DON'T **THINK**—

HOW'S BEN?

DENNIS DIDN'T LIKE IT, BUT HE DID AS JACQUI SAID. BACK AT THE ESTATE, I WAS SURPRISED TO FIND BILL IN HIS OFFICE.

I SUMMARIZED MY TIME IN THE CELL.

YOU DON'T BELIEVE HIM?

IT'S NOT MUCH OF A STORY, BILL.

THINGS LOOK BAD. I'M TRYING NOT TO JUDGE, BUT—

YES, OF COURSE. EVER THE PSYCHOLOGIST.

FORGIVE ME, SON. I'M ON EDGE. YOU'RE CERTAINLY ENTITLED TO YOUR OPINION.

AS MUCH AS I WISH YOU FELT DIFFERENTLY.

BILL, THERE'S A LOT OF HOSTILITY ON THE ISLAND RIGHT NOW. MUCH OF IT AIMED AT THIS PLACE. AT YOU.

MAYBE YOU SHOULD START THINKING ABOUT YOUR OWN INTERESTS A LITTLE.

BILL SEEMED GENUINELY **PERPLEXED** THAT THE ISLAND PEOPLE COULD HOLD ANYTHING AGAINST HIM. OBLIVIOUS TO HIS IMAGE AS CREEPY LORD OF THE MANOR.

I HAD A LITTLE **CHAT** WITH CREEDMAN. I'M MORE CONVINCED THAN EVER THAT HE'S WORKING FOR STASHER-LAYMAN.

JO PICKER HAS SOMETHING TO DO WITH THEM, AS WELL.

WHAT... HOW DO YOU KNOW?

ROBIN SAW LITERATURE IN HER ROOM. SHE'S ALSO FROM WASHINGTON...

...AND SHE WAS HERE **ALONE** THE NIGHT THE ROACHES APPEARED IN OUR ROOM.

I...WE'VE ALREADY ESTABLISHED THAT WAS MY FAULT. LEAVING THE CAGE OPEN...

DO YOU REALLY **REMEMBER** DOING SO, BILL? I THINK SHE'S WORKING FOR THEM, TOO. I WANTED TO WARN YOU...BECAUSE WE'RE **LEAVING**.

ROBIN AND I WILL BE ON THE NEXT BOAT.

BILL REACHED OUT FOR A CHAIR TO SUPPORT HIMSELF, AND MISSED. HE STAGGERED.

CLUMSY OAF!

CLUMSY GODDAMNED OLD FOOL!

"O LET NOT TIME DECEIVE YOU, YOU CANNOT CONQUER TIME. IN THE BURROWS OF THE NIGHTMARE WHERE JUSTICE NAKED IS, TIME WATCHES US FROM THE SHADOW..."

W. H. AUDEN. EINSTEIN WOULD AGREE, DON'T YOU THINK?

OF COURSE, YOU MUST DO WHAT **YOU** THINK BEST.

WE SAT THERE FOR A LONG TIME, LOOKING AWAY FROM EACH OTHER. I THOUGHT ABOUT BILL'S LATEST RIDDLE.

I THOUGHT ABOUT TIME. ABOUT BILL'S PAST, AND WHAT HE FELT WATCHING FROM HIS OWN DARK SHADOWS.

ROBIN AND I WERE READING IN BED WHEN THE AIR TURNED SUDDENLY *HEAVY* AND WE SAW THE SKY CRACK OPEN.

I WAS SHUTTING THE WINDOWS WHEN THE PHONE RANG. MILO.

THINGS ARE *BAD* AND GETTING *WORSE*, BUT WE'RE BOOKED FOR HOME.

YEAH...I STILL WANT TO HEAR WHAT YOU DUG UP.

SO, *GUESS* WHO COVERED THE MARYLAND CANNIBAL CASE FOR THE LOCAL RAG?

GOT IT ON THE *FIRST* GUESS! *CREEDMAN.* HIS NAME WAS ALL OVER THE STORIES UNTIL THE MIDDLE OF THE CASE.

HE GOT REPLACED, AND SEVERAL COPS GOT FIRED. LEAK *SCANDAL.* COPS PROVIDING DETAILS FOR CASH.

WITHIN MONTHS, CREEDMAN STARTS WORKING FOR *STASHER-LAYMAN.* COMMUNICATIONS OFFICER.

I GOT THE NAMES OF THE COPS WHO GOT THE AX: WHITE, TAGG, JOHNSON, HAYGOOD, CERU—

ANDERS HAYGOOD?

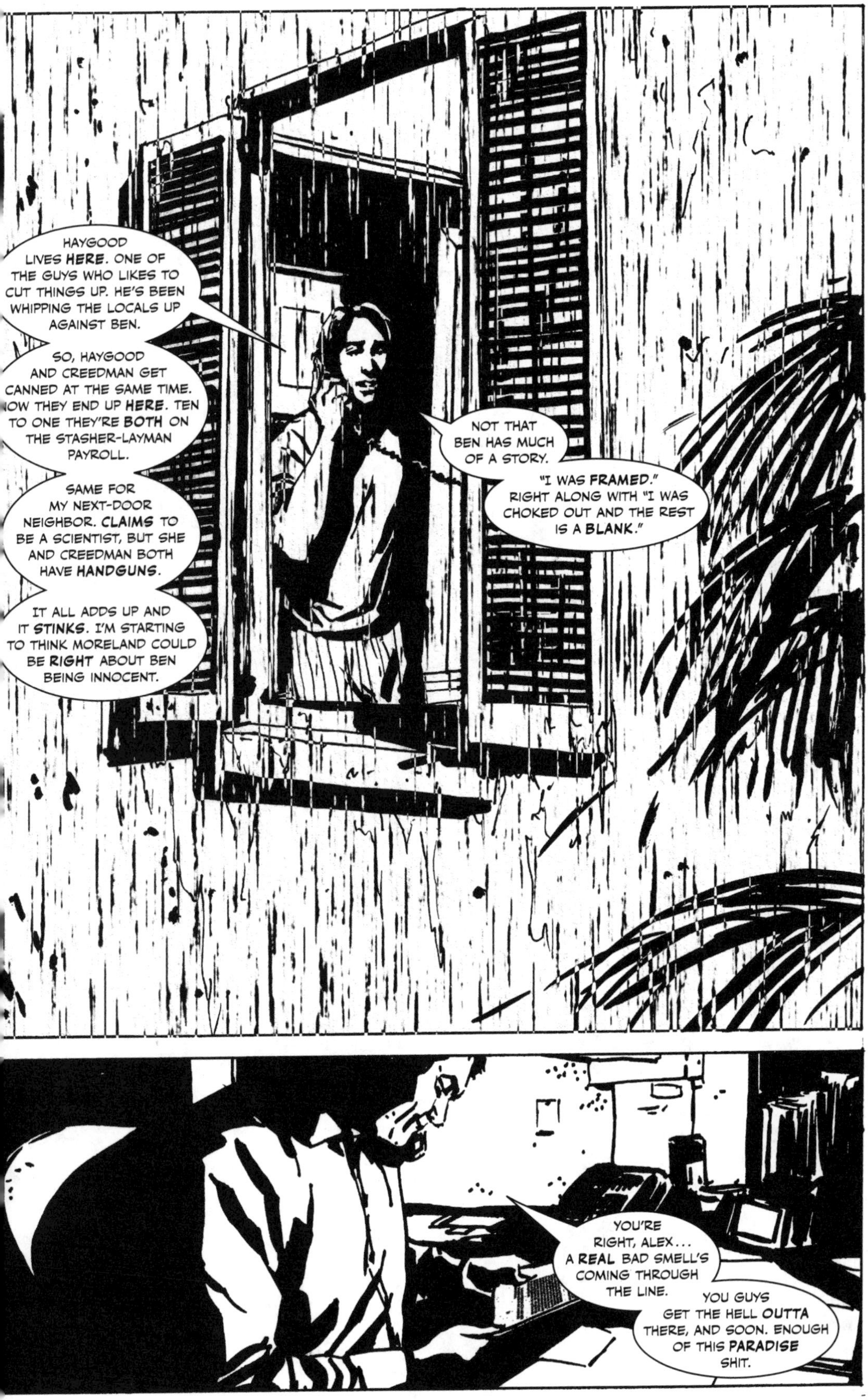
HAYGOOD LIVES HERE. ONE OF THE GUYS WHO LIKES TO CUT THINGS UP. HE'S BEEN WHIPPING THE LOCALS UP AGAINST BEN.
SO, HAYGOOD AND CREEDMAN GET CANNED AT THE SAME TIME. NOW THEY END UP HERE. TEN TO ONE THEY'RE BOTH ON THE STASHER-LAYMAN PAYROLL.
SAME FOR MY NEXT-DOOR NEIGHBOR. CLAIMS TO BE A SCIENTIST, BUT SHE AND CREEDMAN BOTH HAVE HANDGUNS.
IT ALL ADDS UP AND IT STINKS. I'M STARTING TO THINK MORELAND COULD BE RIGHT ABOUT BEN BEING INNOCENT.
NOT THAT BEN HAS MUCH OF A STORY.
"I WAS FRAMED." RIGHT ALONG WITH "I WAS CHOKED OUT AND THE REST IS A BLANK."
YOU'RE RIGHT, ALEX... A REAL BAD SMELL'S COMING THROUGH THE LINE.
YOU GUYS GET THE HELL OUTTA THERE, AND SOON. ENOUGH OF THIS PARADISE SHIT.

AFTER I HUNG UP, THE STORM GATHERED STRENGTH. AS MORE PUZZLE PIECES REVEALED THEMSELVES, I THOUGHT ABOUT WHAT BILL HAD SAID..."*GUILT'S A GREAT MOTIVATOR.*"

ALL THESE YEARS, ALL HIS **ACCOMPLISHMENTS**, ALL OF IT PROPELLED BY A TROUBLED CONSCIENCE? MILO WAS RIGHT. IT WASN'T MY BATTLE.

I TOLD ROBIN WHAT MILO HAD LEARNED.

SO IT'S GOOD WE'RE LEAVING.

IT WAS A DARK AND STORMY NIGHT.

YOU KNOW, ALEX...IT HASN'T BEEN **ALL** BAD.

NOK-NOKK

HAVE YOU SEEN DAD?

WE CAN'T FIND HIM ANY-WHERE.

PAM HAD GONE LOOKING FOR HER FATHER AS THE RAINS HIT. HE WAS **NOWHERE** TO BE FOUND. SHE FEARED HE MIGHT HAVE FALLEN OUTSIDE.

SHE AND JO PICKER WERE SEARCHING THE GROUNDS. JO HAD RAIN GEAR. I WONDERED IF SHE WAS PACKING HER GUN UNDER HER SLICKER.

PAM HAD SAID THERE WERE NO LIGHTS ON IN BILL'S **OFFICE**, BUT I WANTED TO CHECK ANYWAY. IT WAS THE LAST PLACE I'D SEEN HIM, WHEN HE'D FALLEN.

ROBIN INSISTED ON COMING ALONG. WE BRAVED THE RAIN **TOGETHER**.

WE WERE **SOAKED** THROUGH. WE SOUNDED LIKE SQUEEGEES WHEN WE MOVED.

AN OPEN BOOK ON BILL'S DESK. THE OXFORD DICTIONARY OF QUOTATIONS. NOTATIONS ON PAGE 186, IN MORELAND'S HAND.

QUOTES FROM FLAUBERT, IN THE ORIGINAL FRENCH. SORRY, DR. BILL, I TOOK **LATIN** IN HIGH SCHOOL...

I FELT A LUMP IN THE BOOK. TEN PAGES DOWN, TAPED TO THE PAPER, WAS A SHINY BRASS KEY.

UNDER THE KEY WAS ANOTHER HAND-WRITTEN INSCRIPTION, IN LETTERS SO TINY I COULD BARELY MAKE THEM OUT.

"THANK YOU FOR PERSISTING. GUSTAVE'S GIRL WILL BE ASSISTING."

"GUSTAVE'S GIRL?"

GUSTAVE FLAUBERT. THE GIRL THAT COMES TO MIND IS MADAME BOVARY.

MEANING WHAT?

MADAME BOVARY WAS MARRIED TO A DOCTOR. GOT BORED, HAD AFFAIRS, RUINED HER LIFE AND THEN ATE POISON.

A DOCTOR'S WIFE? BARBARA MORELAND? IS BILL TRYING TO TELL US...

THE TRUTH HIT ME NASTILY AND UNEXPECTEDLY, LIKE A DRUNK DRIVER.

NOT HIS WIFE. BOVARY'S FIRST NAME WAS EMMA. ANOTHER EMMA IS GOING TO HELP US.

ONE WITH EIGHT LEGS.

TEN MINUTES LATER WE WERE BACK IN THE INSECTARIUM, AT EMMA'S CAGE.

I DON'T SEE A THING. MAYBE SHE'S NOT—

GAH!

GOOD EVENING, EMMA. STILL AS HUGE AS EVER, I SEE.

ROBIN, YOU SURE ABOUT THIS?

IT'S OKAY, ALEX. BILL SAID SHE'S NOT VENOMOUS.

HE SAID SHE WASN'T VENOMOUS TO KILL PREY, SO SHE CRUSHES IT.

I'M NOT WORRIED.

I HAVE A GOOD FEELING ABOUT HER.

SEE, ALEX? WE'RE BUDDIES. WHY DON'T YOU SEE IF THERE'S ANYTHING IN THE CAGE?

MORELAND HAD INDEED PLACED ANOTHER NOTE IN EMMA'S CAGE. I DIDN'T RELISH ROOTING AROUND FOR IT, EVEN IF EMMA WASN'T HOME.

BILL'S GAMES WERE WEARING ON ME.

"IMPRESSIVE THOUGH EMMA MAY BE AT FIRST SIGHT, EVERYTHING'S RELATIVE—SIZE AS WELL AS TIME."

I KNEW WHAT HE MEANT INSTANTLY. WE WERE TO LOOK FOR THE NEXT CLUE IN THE CENTIPEDE'S CAGE.

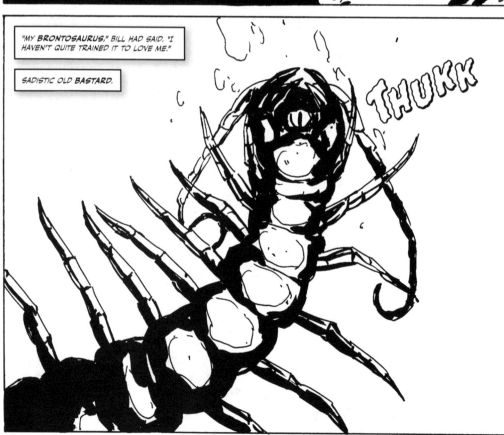

"MY BRONTOSAURUS," BILL HAD SAID. "I HAVEN'T QUITE TRAINED IT TO LOVE ME."

SADISTIC OLD BASTARD.

THUKK

THUNNG

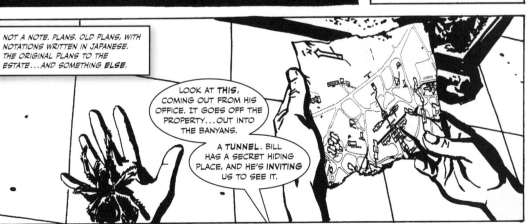

NOT A NOTE. PLANS. OLD PLANS, WITH NOTATIONS WRITTEN IN JAPANESE. THE ORIGINAL PLANS TO THE ESTATE...AND SOMETHING ELSE.

THE MAP LED US **BACK** TO BILL'S OFFICE, AND THEN TO HIS LAB. TEN MINUTES LATER, WE'D MOVED THE TABLE THAT COVERED THE TRAPDOOR AND FOUND THE PRESSURE POINT THAT OPENED IT.

OLD PULLEYS AND GEARS, BUT WELL-OILED AND EFFICIENT.

GUESS THIS IS WHY THEY CALL SPIES **MOLES**.

THE DIRT FLOOR AND CONCRETE WALLS WERE COMPLETELY **DRY**. A PERFECT SEAL.

THE RAILROAD TRACK WAS TOO SMALL FOR ANY TRAIN. MUST HAVE BEEN FOR A HANDCAR, BUT NONE WAS IN SIGHT.

CRYPTIC MESSAGES, BUGS, TRAPDOORS...HE'S LIKE A BIG KID PLAYING **GAMES**. WE COULD WAIT UNTIL **MORNING**.

WE'VE COME **THIS** FAR, ALEX. HE'S DOWN HERE. HE CLEARLY WANTS **US** DOWN HERE.

WHY WOULD HE WANT TO **HURT** US?

ALL RIGHT. LET'S **PLAY**.

A FEW HUNDRED PACES IN, THE MONOTONY OF THE TUNNEL WAS...**PLEASANT.** WARM, DRY AND SILENT.

WHAT DO YOU THINK IT WAS **ORIGINALLY?** AN ESCAPE ROUTE FOR THE JAPANESE?

OR SOME KIND OF **SUPPLY** CHANNEL.

THE BOXES CONTAINED DRIED FRUITS AND VEGETABLES, PHARMACEUTICALS LIKE ANTIBIOTICS AND DIETARY SUPPLEMENTS, TONIC WATER AND GATORADE.

SOME OF THE STUFF WAS NAVY ISSUE. DATED **1963.**

THIRTY YEARS! HE MUST BE DAMNED PROUD. NOW HE WANTS TO SHOW IT OFF.

AS WE PASSED THROUGH OUR FIRST DOORWAY, THE LIGHTING BEHIND US FADED TO **DARKNESS** AHEAD.

KRANNG

DAMN YOU, BILL!

125

I DIDN'T *SCREAM.* SOMEHOW I ALMOST SMILED BACK AT...*HIM?*

THE HAND FELL AWAY FROM MY SHOULDER, THE FINGERS CURLING IN A WAY NORMAL FINGERS COULDN'T.

SERPENTINE. NO...EVEN A *SNAKE* HAD MORE FIRMNESS. WHITE AND FLACCID. *WORMLIKE.*

HI.

WE *FOLLOWED* THEM THROUGH WHAT HAD BECOME A VAST, DIM CAVE. ROBIN AND I STUMBLED OVER BITS OF ROCK.

THE LITTLE SOFT MEN HAD NO TROUBLE AT ALL.

EVERYTHING NEAT. *CLEAN.* THE DISTANT HUM OF A GENERATOR WAS AUDIBLE.

THE RAIN WAS AUDIBLE NOW. A TINKLE. BUT EVERYTHING WAS DRY.

FINALLY, THE ENGINEER OF OUR NIGHT'S ADVENTURE SHOWED UP. FOUR MORE PEOPLE CAME WITH HIM, INCLUDING TWO WOMEN.

ALEX, ROBIN... WELCOME.

IT'S ALL RIGHT, CHILDREN. DON'T BE FRIGHTENED. THEY'RE GOOD.

REMEMBER TO DRINK NOW. THAT'S GOOD.

SORRY TO PUT YOU THROUGH THIS RIGAMAROLE...BOTH OF YOU. ROBIN, I'M SO GLAD YOU CAME, DEAR.

NOW I KNEW THE SOURCE OF BILL'S EXHAUSTION. ALL THOSE NIGHTS SPENT CARING FOR THEM. ALL THOSE YEARS, BARELY SLEEPING.

I LOOKED AT THE WHITE FACES AROUND US. THE DEFORMED BODIES.

JOSEPH CRISTOBAL HAD SEEN SOMETHING LIKE THIS.

THE PIECES FALLING INTO PLACE LIKE THE TUMBLERS OF A LOCK. MORE OF BILL'S LIES SLOWLY UNRAVELING.

FINISHED? GOOD. NOW PLEASE CLEAR YOUR PLATES AND GO TO THE GAME ROOM FOR SOME FUN.

THEY'RE SO GENTLE. THE GENTLEST PEOPLE I KNOW.

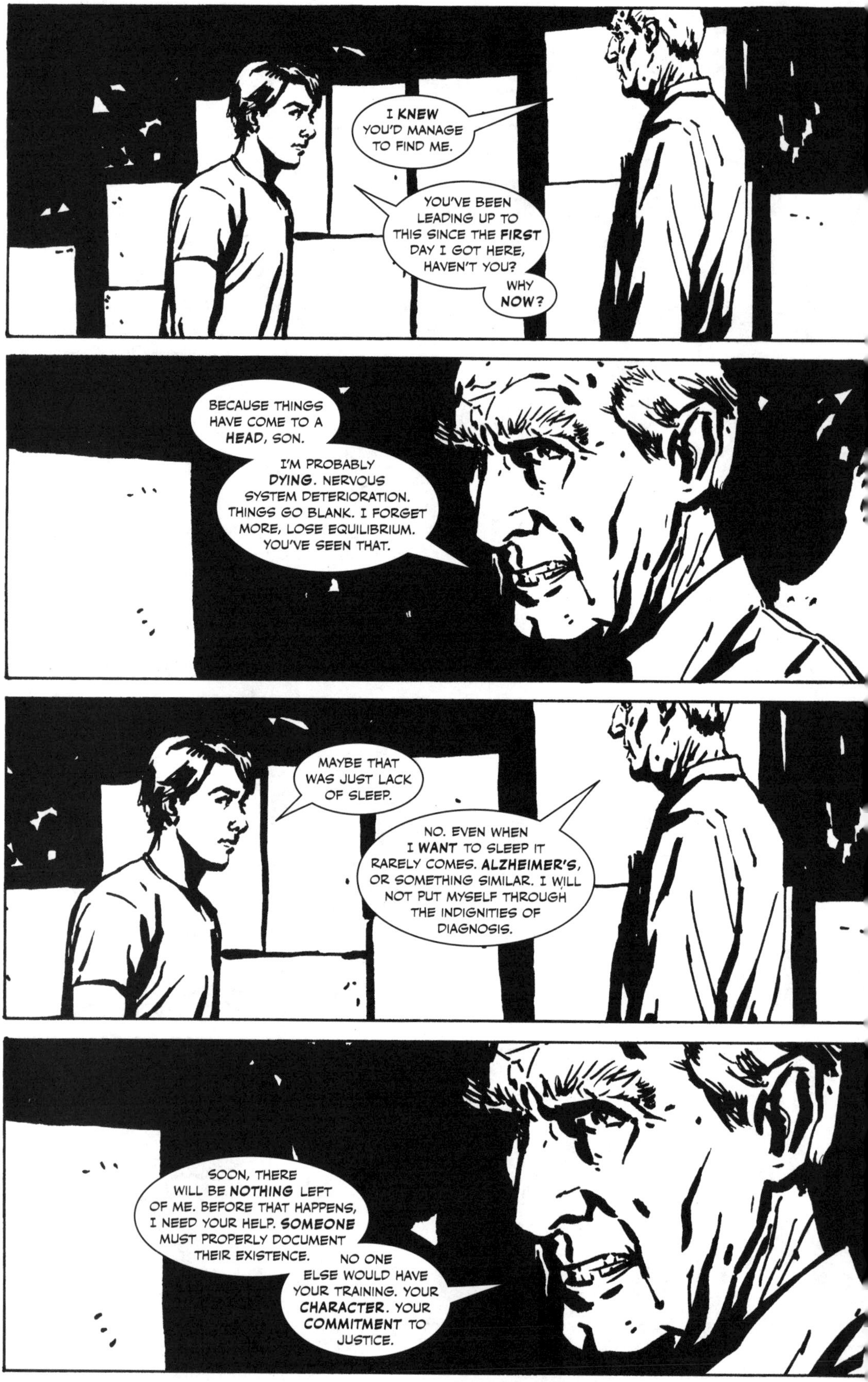
I KNEW YOU'D MANAGE TO FIND ME.
YOU'VE BEEN LEADING UP TO THIS SINCE THE FIRST DAY I GOT HERE, HAVEN'T YOU?
WHY NOW?
BECAUSE THINGS HAVE COME TO A HEAD, SON.
I'M PROBABLY DYING. NERVOUS SYSTEM DETERIORATION. THINGS GO BLANK. I FORGET MORE, LOSE EQUILIBRIUM. YOU'VE SEEN THAT.
MAYBE THAT WAS JUST LACK OF SLEEP.
NO. EVEN WHEN I WANT TO SLEEP IT RARELY COMES. ALZHEIMER'S, OR SOMETHING SIMILAR. I WILL NOT PUT MYSELF THROUGH THE INDIGNITIES OF DIAGNOSIS.
SOON, THERE WILL BE NOTHING LEFT OF ME. BEFORE THAT HAPPENS, I NEED YOUR HELP. SOMEONE MUST PROPERLY DOCUMENT THEIR EXISTENCE.
NO ONE ELSE WOULD HAVE YOUR TRAINING. YOUR CHARACTER. YOUR COMMITMENT TO JUSTICE.

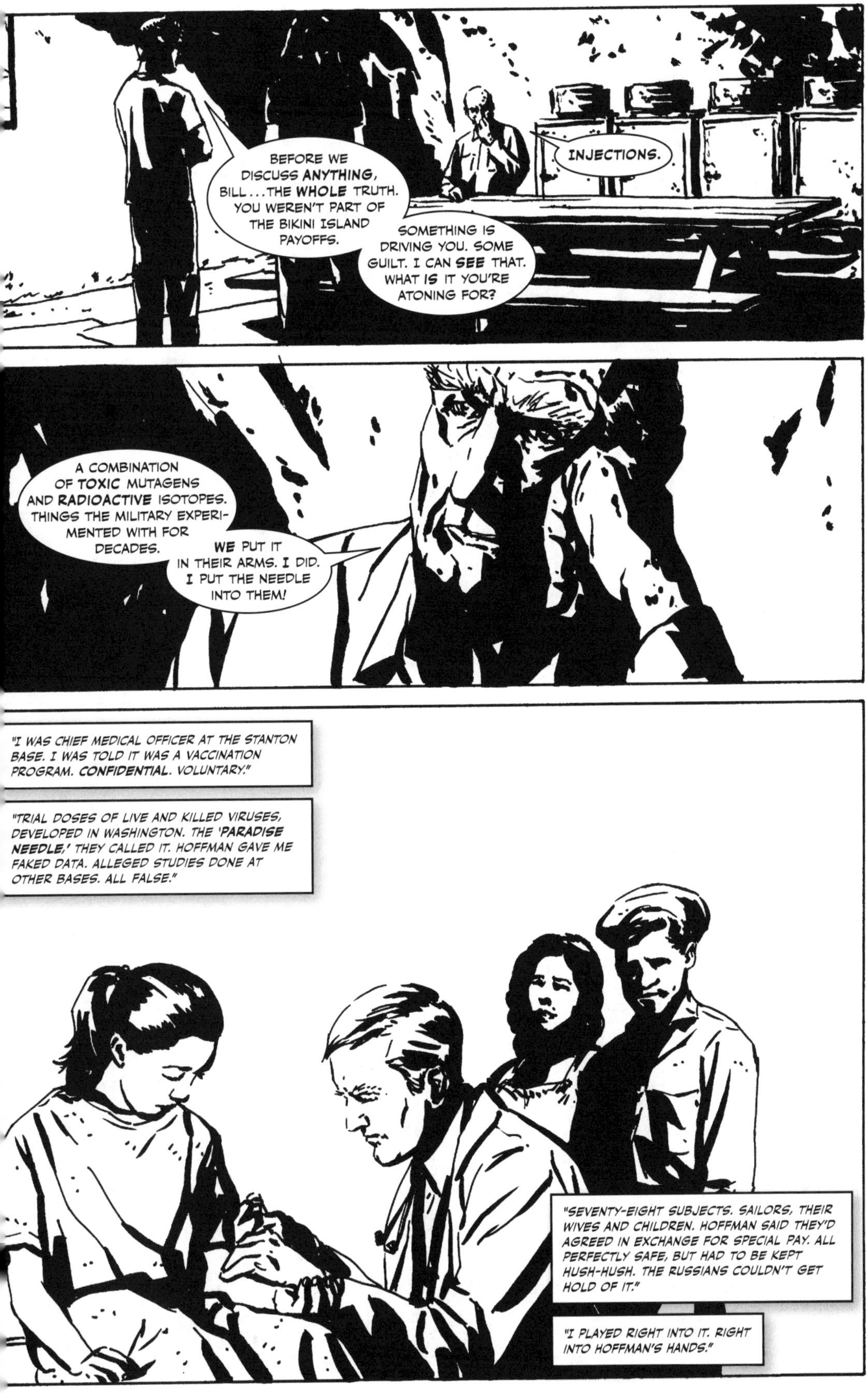

BEFORE WE DISCUSS **ANYTHING**, BILL . . . THE **WHOLE** TRUTH. YOU WEREN'T PART OF THE BIKINI ISLAND PAYOFFS.
SOMETHING IS DRIVING YOU. SOME GUILT. I CAN **SEE** THAT. WHAT **IS** IT YOU'RE ATONING FOR?
INJECTIONS.
A COMBINATION OF **TOXIC** MUTAGENS AND **RADIOACTIVE** ISOTOPES. THINGS THE MILITARY EXPERIMENTED WITH FOR DECADES.
WE PUT IT IN THEIR ARMS. **I** DID. **I** PUT THE NEEDLE INTO THEM!
"I WAS CHIEF MEDICAL OFFICER AT THE STANTON BASE. I WAS TOLD IT WAS A VACCINATION PROGRAM. **CONFIDENTIAL**. VOLUNTARY."
"TRIAL DOSES OF LIVE AND KILLED VIRUSES, DEVELOPED IN WASHINGTON. THE '**PARADISE NEEDLE**,' THEY CALLED IT. HOFFMAN GAVE ME FAKED DATA. ALLEGED STUDIES DONE AT OTHER BASES. ALL FALSE."
"SEVENTY-EIGHT SUBJECTS. SAILORS, THEIR WIVES AND CHILDREN. HOFFMAN SAID THEY'D AGREED IN EXCHANGE FOR SPECIAL PAY. ALL PERFECTLY SAFE, BUT HAD TO BE KEPT HUSH-HUSH. THE RUSSIANS COULDN'T GET HOLD OF IT."
"I PLAYED RIGHT INTO IT. RIGHT INTO HOFFMAN'S HANDS."

"IN '63, I WAS MONTHS AWAY FROM DISCHARGE. WE'D FALLEN IN LOVE WITH *ARUK*. HOFFMAN OFFERED US THE ESTATE AT A BARGAIN PRICE..."

"...IN EXCHANGE FOR MY *SILENCE* ABOUT THE VACCINATION PROGRAM."

"BLISSFUL, STUPID *IGNORANCE* UNTIL A MONTH LATER. ONE OF THE WOMEN WHO'D BEEN INJECTED GAVE BIRTH."

"I'D ASKED HOFFMAN ABOUT INJECTING A PREGNANT WOMAN. HE *ASSURED* ME IT WAS SAFE. HIS BOGUS STUDIES PROVED AS MUCH."

THAT *BABY*...NO BRAIN, LIMP AS A JELLYFISH. IT REMINDED ME OF THINGS I'D SEEN ON THE MARSHALLS.

NEXT CAME A SAILOR. A RARE TUMOR. THE RAPIDITY WAS ASTONISHING. IT STARTED TO HIT ME THEN, WITH *FULL* FORCE. I KNEW THE SYMPTOMS OF *RADIATION* POISONING.

I'M SORRY I *LIED* ABOUT THE PAYMENTS. TRYING TO COUCH MY OWN *GUILT*, I SUPPOSE.

I WENT TO HOFFMAN. HE JUST **SMILED**. THAT SAME SMILE HE FLASHED WHEN HE CHEATED AT CARDS AND THOUGHT HE WAS GETTING AWAY WITH IT.

HE HAD THE RECORDS **PURGED**. THE BODIES TAKEN AWAY BEFORE I COULD PERFORM AUTOPSIES. THEN, I HEARD ALL THE VACCINATED FAMILIES WERE BEING SHIPPED TO WALTER REED. I **KNEW** WHAT THAT MEANT.

"I SNEAKED INTO THE INFIRMARY ONE NIGHT. ONLY ONE ATTENDANT WAS ON GUARD."

"MY GOD..."

"SOME WERE ALREADY **DEAD**. JUST LYING THERE...ROTTING. OTHERS WERE BARELY HOLDING ON. SLOUGHED SKIN WAS EVERYWHERE. LIMBS...THE ROOM STANK OF GANGRENE."

"BED AFTER BED, **CRAMMED** TOGETHER LIKE COFFINS. NO ATTEMPT BEING MADE TO TREAT THEM. NO FOOD. NO MEDICATION OR IV LINES."

IN ANOTHER WARD I FOUND THE **CHILDREN**, MOST OF THEM ALREADY DEAD. THEN... A **MIRACLE**.

SOME OF THE BABIES WERE STILL **ALIVE**. DERMAL LESIONS, MALNUTRITION, BUT CONSCIOUS. THEIR LITTLE EYES **FOLLOWED** ME AS I STOOD OVER THEIR CRIBS. I COUNTED. NINE.

I GOT THEM OUT, SWADDLED IN BLANKETS TO MUFFLE THEIR CRIES. I NEEDN'T HAVE BOTHERED. THE VACCINE HAD BURNED THEIR VOCAL CORDS AWAY.

I'D DISCOVERED THE CAVES WHILE HIKING. IT SEEMED THE ONLY SAFE PLACE. THEN... A **COMPLICATION**.

"HE'D BEEN A MECHANIC AT THE BASE. A LARGE MAN, AND NOT A KIND ONE. HE WAS **ENRAGED**...CONFUSED BY HIS CONDITION."

"I WAS AFRAID HE'D SET OFF AN ALARM. I SAW NO CHOICE BUT TO SNEAK HIM OUT, TOO. IT TOOK ALL MY STRENGTH TO **CONTROL HIM**."

"I DIDN'T THINK HE'D LAST LONG, BUT HE MADE IT FIVE DAYS, LUNGING AROUND THE CAVES. **FLAILING**, INJURING HIMSELF. ON THE FIFTH DAY, HE **ESCAPED**."

JOSEPH CRISTOBAL **SAW** HIM.

YES. HE WAS CLAIMING HE'D SEEN SOME KIND OF FOREST DEVIL. I **CREATED** THE A. TUTALO STORY.

TOOTALI IS THE OLD WORD FOR "GRUB." THERE IS NO SUCH **MYTH.**

YOU LET HIM KEEP **BELIEVING** HE'D SEEN A MONSTER. DID IT CONTRIBUTE TO HIS **DEATH?**

WHAT **SHOULD** I HAVE DONE, SON? TOLD HIM EVERYTHING? ENDANGERED THE BABIES? **THEY WERE** MY PRIORITY.

JOSEPH ALWAYS WAS SUCH A **STUBBORN** MAN ...

WEEKS LATER, A NAVY TRANSPORT **EXPLODED** OVER THE OCEAN AFTER TAKEOFF. PATIENTS, DOCTORS, GUARDS. ALL **GONE.** HOFFMAN ELIMINATING ANY WITNESSES.

MY GOD.

WHY WEREN'T **YOU** ELIMINATED?

I'D BOUGHT MY-SELF SOME **INSURANCE.** THE DAY OF THE CRASH I'D INVITED HOFFMAN OVER FOR DRINKS. I TOLD HIM I KNEW **EXACTLY** WHAT HE'D DONE.

I SAID I HAD HIDDEN A DETAILED RECORD OF **EVERYTHING,** WITH INSTRUCTIONS TO MAKE IT PUBLIC IF ANYTHING HAPPENED TO ME OR MY FAMILY.

HOFFMAN JUST SMILED THAT SMILE OF HIS AND ASKED FOR ANOTHER DRINK. BUT WE **WERE** LEFT ALONE.

WE MET **SIX** JUST NOW. IS THAT ALL OF THEM?

WHAT'S THEIR HEALTH STATUS, PHYSICALLY AND MENTALLY?

YES...SIX **SURVIVED.**

NONE OF THEM HAVE NORMAL **INTELLIGENCE,** AND THEY HAVE NO SPEECH. THEIR IQ'S RANGE FROM FIFTY TO SIXTY.

THEIR NERVOUS SYSTEMS ARE GROSSLY AB-NORMAL.

EXTREME PHOTOSENSITIVITY... THE SLIGHTEST BIT OF UV EATS UP THEIR SKIN.

THEY'RE **STERILE.** A BLESSING, I SUPPOSE. NOT MUCH LIBIDO, EITHER **THAT'S** MADE LIFE EASIER.

I STILL DON'T SEE HOW YOU'VE MANAGED TO **KEEP** THEM DOWN HERE ALL THESE YEARS.

AT FIRST IT WAS DIFFICULT, SON. I HAD TO CONFINE THEM. **NOW**... WELL, THEY MAY NOT BE NORMAL, BUT THEY'VE LEARNED WHAT THE SUN DOES TO THEM.

I'VE MADE EVERY EFFORT TO PROVIDE THEM WITH AS **RICH** A LIFE AS POS-SIBLE. HERE...

*"...LET ME **SHOW** YOU."*

*BILL'S **"CHILDREN"** AT PLAY. HE'D MADE A COMFORTABLE HOME FOR THEM IN THE CAVES. BEANBAG CHAIRS, SHAG CARPETING. A RECORD PLAYER. BURL IVES SINGING "JIMMY CRACK CORN."*

THEY ALL LOOKED CONTENT. *HAPPY*. EVEN *BILL*...IN THE MOMENTS HE WAS PLAYING WITH THEM HE LOOKED A DECADE YOUNGER.

ALL THESE YEARS, VIRTUALLY *NO* SLEEP. SENDING HIS OWN DAUGHTER AWAY AS A TODDLER.

LOOK, SUZY...MOVIE STAR BARBIE. LOOK AT THIS *FANCY* DRESS.

ALLOWING THE ISLAND TO DECAY. THE *INSECTS* HIS ONLY RECREATION...A SMALL WORLD HE COULD CONTROL. STUDYING PREDATORS TO FORGET ABOUT VICTIMS.

COME, PLEASE...I'LL SHOW YOU THE *REST* OF OUR LITTLE WORLD.

BILL LED US THROUGH BEDROOMS AND BATHROOMS. AFTER ANOTHER IRON DOOR WE STOOD UNDER NATURAL LIGHT FROM ABOVE.

SOMETIMES AT NIGHT, WHEN I *KNOW* THEY'LL BEHAVE, I TAKE THEM UP TO THE JUNGLE FOR PICNICS. THE MOONLIGHT IS KIND TO THEM.

DO YOU HAVE ANY IDEA OF THEIR LIFE EXPECTANCY?

WITH GOOD CARE, THEY'LL PROBABLY ALL OUTLIVE ME. *THAT* IS THE ISSUE. I MUST...*ARRANGE* SOMETHING FOR THEM.

THEY NEED *CONTINUITY*. A TRANSFER OF CARE. I WANT YOU TO BE THEIR *GUARDIANS* ONCE I'M GONE.

MY MIND **REELED.** SOMEWHERE IN THE DISTANCE THE RECORD PLAYER SKIPPED NEAR THE END OF "SKIP TO MY LOU."

HEAR ME OUT. DON'T CLOSE YOUR MINDS. **PLEASE.**

I'M NOT PROPOSING A ONE-WAY DEAL. CARE FOR MY KIDS PROPERLY, AND THE ENTIRE **ESTATE** WILL BE YOURS.

MY HOLDINGS MAY NOT BE WORTH WHAT THEY ONCE WERE, BUT THERE'S **SIGNIFICANT** LAND. SOME SECURITIES AND CASH.

I'LL LEAVE PAM A GENEROUS INHERITANCE. THE **REST** WOULD BE YOURS.

BEN WILL **HELP.** HE CAN—

BEN **KNOWS?**

I TOLD HIM YEARS AGO.

THE KIDS HAVE COME TO **ADORE** HIM, BUT HE HAS HIS OWN FAMILY. THEY NEED **FULL-TIME** PARENTS.

WHY NOT PAM?

SHE'S A **WONDERFUL** GIRL, BUT NOT EQUIPPED. SHE HAS... **VULNERABIL-ITIES.**

MY FAULT. I HARDLY **DESERVE** THE TITLE "FATHER." SHE NEEDS TO FIND SOME-ONE...THE KIND OF RELATIONSHIP YOU TWO HAVE.

PLEASE. **ACCEPT** MY OFFER. I'M AT YOUR **MERCY.**

A WOMAN'S TOUCH WOULD BE SO GOOD FOR THEM. NOW THAT YOU KNOW **EVERYTHING—**

DO WE, BILL?

WHAT'S THE **PROBLEM**, SON?

HOFFMAN. I THINK THERE'S **MORE** TO YOUR DETENTE.

I THINK YOU TWO ARE **LOCKED** TOGETHER, LIKE **RAMS** WITH TWISTED HORNS.

HE CAN'T MOVE IN AND DESTROY ARUK **OVERNIGHT**, BUT HE ALSO KNOWS YOU CAN'T EXPOSE HIM BECAUSE OF SOMETHING **HE** KNOWS.

SO, HE WEARS YOU DOWN **SLOWLY.** WITH STASHER-LAYMAN RIGHT BEHIND HIM.

THEY WANT TO PUT A **PRISON** ON ARUK, DON'T THEY?

VERY GOOD, SON. **YES.** HE WANTS TO CALL IT "PARADISE ISLAND." CLEVER, NO?

THERE'S EVEN **MORE.** HE WANTS TO ALLOW THE **DUMPING** OF RADIOACTIVE WASTE IN THE SURROUNDING WATERS.

WHAT **ELSE,** BILL? IF HE HAS NOTHING ON YOU, HOW CAN HE MAKE THESE MOVES? WHY DON'T YOU HAVE MORE POWER?

WHAT'S HE HOLDING **OVER** YOU?

NO...THERE'S **NOTHING.** MY OFFER...

FINE. YOU'RE ENTITLED TO YOUR PRIVACY. GOOD-BYE, BILL.

PLEASE! EVERYTHING IN DUE TIME! I'M OFFERING YOU A CHANCE TO ENRICH YOUR LIVES!

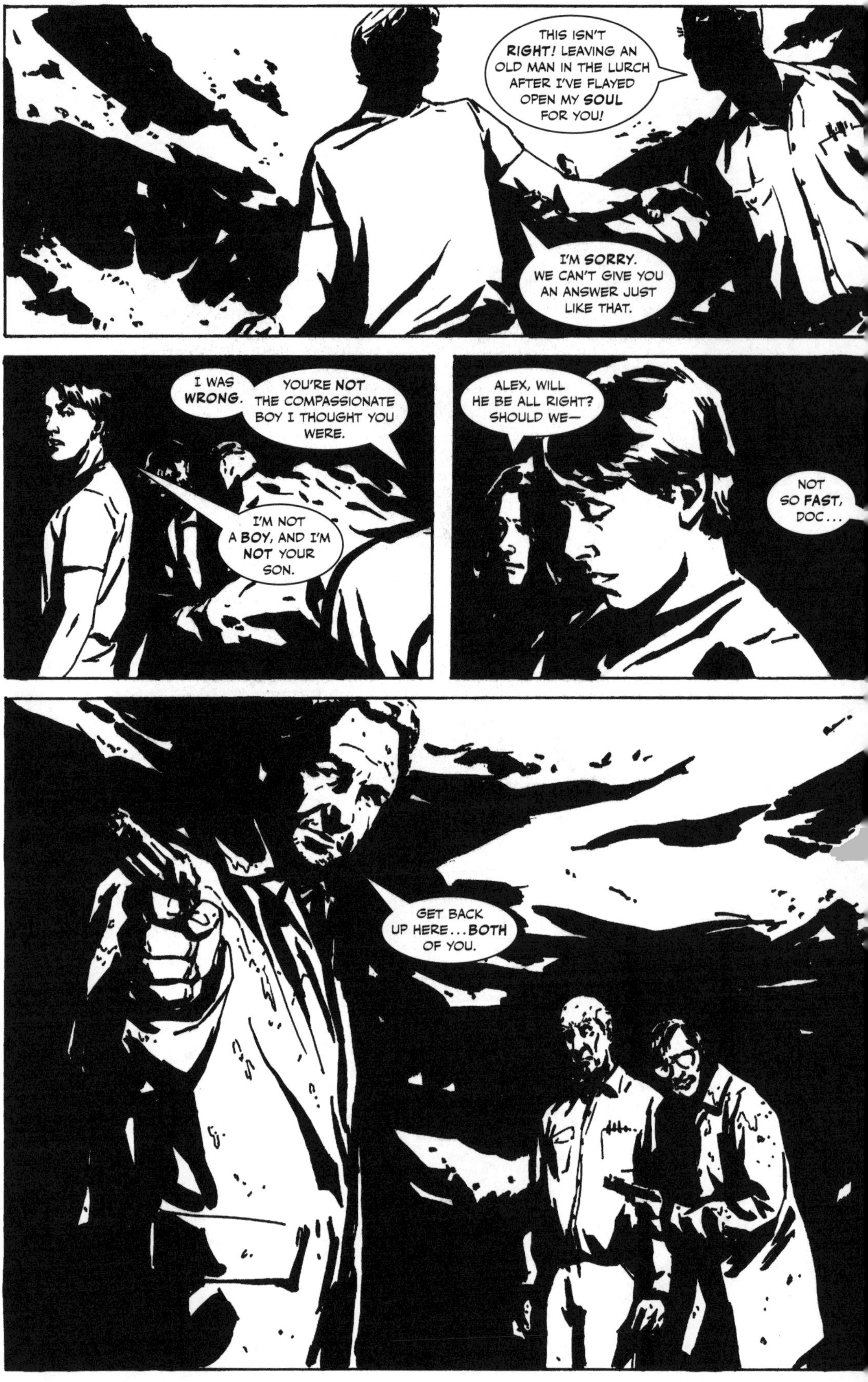
THIS ISN'T RIGHT! LEAVING AN OLD MAN IN THE LURCH AFTER I'VE FLAYED OPEN MY SOUL FOR YOU!
I'M SORRY. WE CAN'T GIVE YOU AN ANSWER JUST LIKE THAT.
I WAS WRONG.
YOU'RE NOT THE COMPASSIONATE BOY I THOUGHT YOU WERE.
I'M NOT A BOY, AND I'M NOT YOUR SON.
ALEX, WILL HE BE ALL RIGHT? SHOULD WE—
NOT SO FAST, DOC...
GET BACK UP HERE...BOTH OF YOU.

HAYGOOD FRISKED US WITH THE PRACTICED BOREDOM OF AN EX-COP. HIS HANDS LINGERED NEAR ROBIN'S CROTCH, **PROBING**. SHE TRIED NOT TO SCREAM. I TRIED TO PULL HIS ATTENTION AWAY FROM HER.

THE BOYS FROM **MARYLAND**, OFF ON A SOUTH SEAS LARK.

C'MON.

SO, WHY'D YOU PULL US OVER, **OFFICER?**

NEVER MET A CANNIBAL BEFORE. WHO DID THE SURGERY, OR WAS IT **BOTH** OF YOU?

FUCK OFF.

CHILL.

LET'S GO.

AS WE WALKED THE RAIN ABOVE GOT **LOUDER**. THEY'D OPENED SOME KIND OF HATCH ABOVEGROUND.

THEY'D LIKELY **FOUND** THE TUNNELS BECAUSE OF ALL THE OPEN DOORS I'D LEFT BEHIND.

SO...REPORTER BUYS MURDER INFO FROM COP IN MARYLAND, AND NOW THEY'RE RE-**UNITED** BY GOOD OL' STASHER-LAYMAN.

DOES THE COMPANY KNOW YOU REPLICATED THE **MURDER** THAT GOT YOU IN TROUBLE IN THE FIRST PLACE?

SLICING UP WOMEN AND PRETENDING TO EAT THEM. OR...MAYBE **NOT**. YOU DID SAY YOU WERE A GOURMET CHEF, TOM.

GOT A RECIPE YOU CAN SHARE? GIRL BOURGUIGNON?

THAT'S **ENOUGH**. KEEP MOVING.

WHAT DO YOU HAVE DOWN HERE?

MY LITTLE **SANCTUARY**. OLD FURNITURE, CLOTHES, A FEW BOOKS. NOTHING **INTERESTING**.

LET'S TAKE A LOOK ANYWAY.

DON'T **SURPRISE** ME, DOCTOR. YOU GO AHEAD. TOM...

...ANYTHING HAPPENS, **KILL** THE GIRL.

AS THEY LED US CLOSER TO THE GAME ROOM, A SOUND: MUSIC. "THE WHEELS ON THE BUS GO ROUND AND ROUND..."

WHAT'S WITH THE MUSIC?

KIDDIE MUSIC? YOU ARE ONE BUGGY OLD FART.

YOU BRING LITTLE KIDS DOWN HERE TO PLAY "DOCTOR"?

PROJECTION.

PROJECTION? WHAT THE HELL ARE YOU—

A FREUDIAN TERM. PROJECTING ONE'S OWN IMPULSES ONTO ANOTHER. THAT'S WHAT YOU JUST DID.

OH, FUCK OFF, YOU SELF-RIGHTEOUS BAG OF SHIT.

BET YOU ALL DIDN'T KNOW DR. BILL HERE WAS ONCE THE ACE PUSSY-HOUND OF THE U.S. NAVY.

CHASED EVERYTHING IN A SKIRT: YOUNG, OLD, DARK MEAT...ANY KIND OF MEAT. NICE BEING A DOC, TOO. COULD DO HIS OWN ABORTIONS.

DROVE POOR MRS. BILL TO ONE-WAY SURFING. TURNED HERSELF INTO SHARK CHUM OVER IT.

TOM, KEEP YOUR GUN ON THE GIRL'S HEAD. ANY **TROUBLE**, I WANT TO SEE HER **BRAINS** ON THE WALL.

ENOUGH OF THIS CRAP. I'LL CHECK THESE DOORS.

WAIT!

IT'S **RIGGED**... THAT DOOR AND THE OTHERS. HE'S GOT THEM ALL BOOBY-TRAPPED.

HE **IS** NUTS. STOCKPILING FOOD AND SURVIVAL GEAR, PREPAR-ING FOR THE END OF THE WORLD.

I'D LET YOU BLOW YOURSELF UP, BUT HE'S GOT ENOUGH EXPLOSIVES TO TURN US **ALL** INTO SOUP.

TELL THEM, BILL.

UTTER **NONSENSE**.

THE MUSIC PLAYED, "THE DRIVER ON THE BUS SAYS MOVE ON BACK..."

HE ONLY SHOWED US THAT TRAP...**DYNAMITE** AND A WIRE TO THE DOOR, BUT HE SAID THEY'RE **ALL** RIGGED.

HOW 'BOUT
YOU OPEN THAT
DOOR?

I'D
RATHER
NOT.

MOVE,
YOU CRAZY
ASSHOLE!

THIS IS
SILLY. I'LL
DO NO SUCH
THING.

WHY DON'T WE
JUST **SHOOT** THEM ALL
AND GET THE HELL OUT
OF HERE, ANDERS?

I DON'T
THINK SO.

HAYGOOD HAD BEEN ORDERED TO KEEP
MORELAND ALIVE...*UNTIL HIS INSURANCE
POLICY AGAINST HOFFMAN WAS FOUND.*

*HOFFMAN HAD PLAYED ALONG WITH THIS
LITTLE STALEMATE FOR **THIRTY** YEARS.
HE WAS WILLING TO WAIT A LITTLE
LONGER.*

*STASHER-LAYMAN, PULLING STRINGS TO
REMAKE ARUK AS A PRISON AND NUCLEAR
DUMP. THE PROFITS WOULD BE HUGE.
HOFFMAN WOULD GET HIS TASTE, AS
WOULD HAYGOOD AND CREEDMAN...AND
JO PICKER? HAD EVEN LYMAN'S PLANE
CRASH BEEN PART OF THE PLAN? HAD HIS
BIG MOUTH OFFENDED THE HIGHER-UPS?*

ACTUALLY, HE
DOES HAVE SOME
KIDS DOWN HERE.

WANT TO
SEE?

KIDS! KIDS! **KIDS!**

VERY FUNNY. ALL RIGHT... LET'S MOVE.

WHAT THE HOLY—?

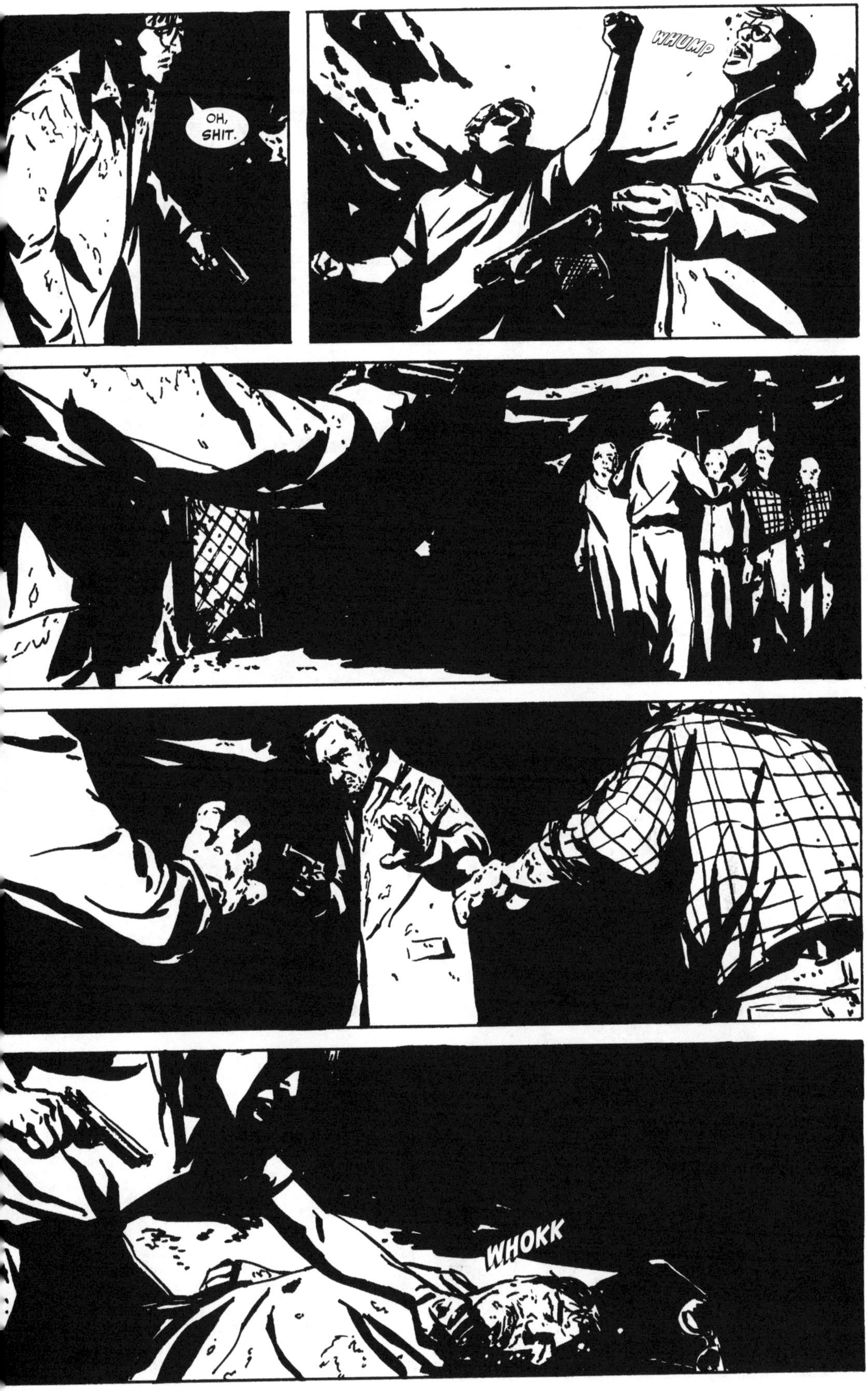
OH, SHIT.
WHUMP
WHOKK

I GRABBED CREEDMAN'S GUN AND ROSE, LOOKING FOR HAYGOOD.

MORELAND'S CHILDREN BLOCKED MY VIEW. THEY GATHERED AROUND BILL AS HE STRUGGLED TO HIS FEET.

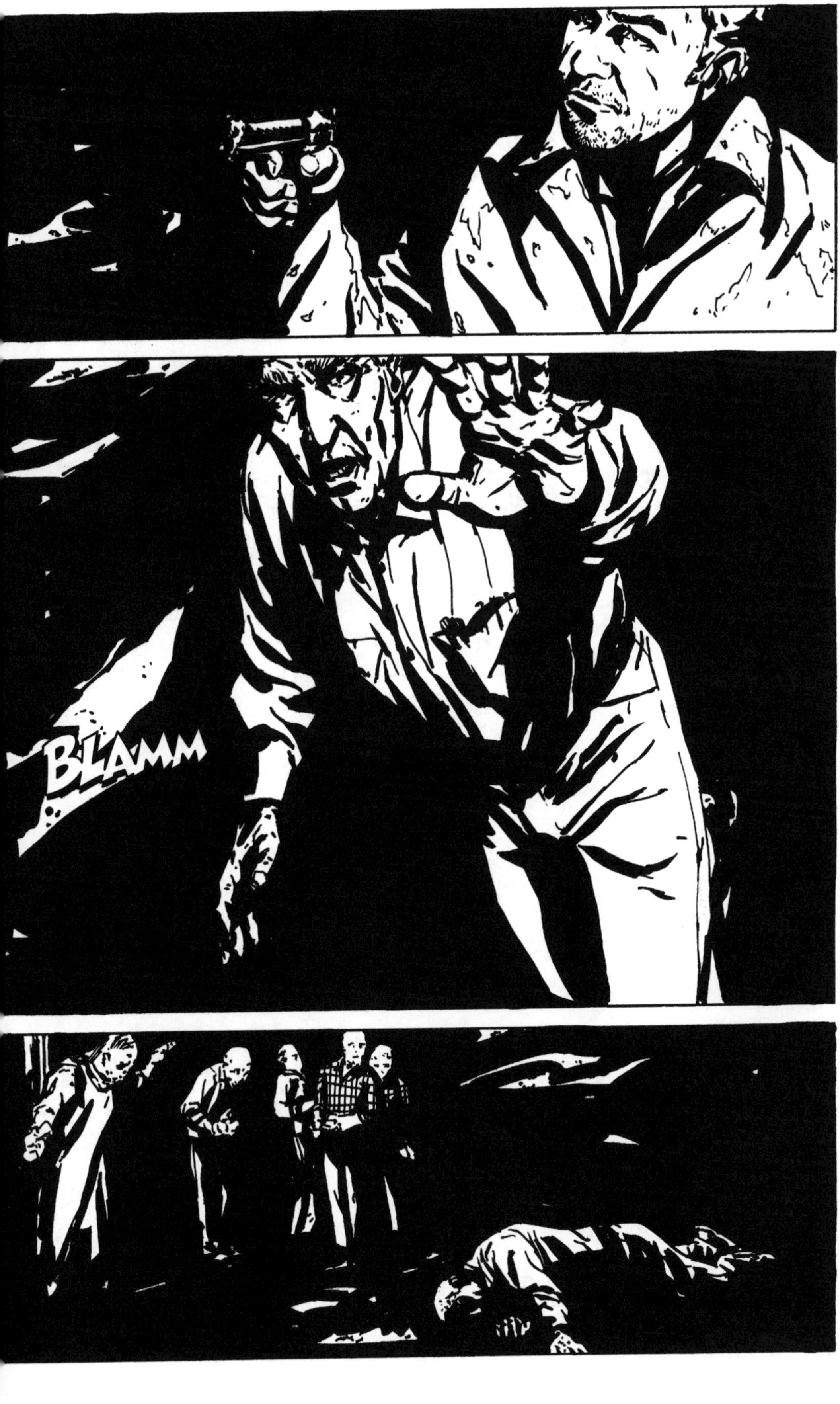
BLAMM

AFTER SHOOTING MORELAND, HAYGOOD SPUN, LOOKING FOR HIS OTHER TARGETS: ROBIN AND ME.

BRAM-
BLAMM

HE WAS TOO LATE.

BLAM-
BRAM-
BRAMM

I'D NEVER OWNED A GUN. NEVER IMAGINED KILLING ANYONE...

...MUCH LESS WITH ROBIN WATCHING.

BILL!

IT'S ALL RIGHT, DEAR. WENT THROUGH THE MUSCLE.

I'M LEAKING, NOT SPURTING, SO THE BRACHIAL ARTERY IS INTACT.

A LITTLE BOOBOO, EDDIE. DADDY'S GOING TO BE JUST FINE.

WE SHOULD GET OUT OF HERE, ALEX.

YES...

WHERE IS JO, TOM? WAITING FOR US UP THERE?

HE DIDN'T RESPOND. OR COULDN'T. HAD I HIT HIM TOO HARD?

WE CAN'T STAY PUT WITH YOU BLEEDING. ANY OTHER WAY OUT, BILL?

JUST THE TWO YOU'VE SEEN TONIGHT. THE RAMP TO THE JUNGLE AND THE TUNNEL TO MY OFFICE.

I PREFER THE OFFICE TO THE DARK JUNGLE. TOM CAN LEAD. IF JO IS WAITING FOR US AT THE HATCH, HE CAN BE HER FIRST COURSE.

THE RETURN TRIP SEEMED A LOT QUICKER. MORELAND MAINTAINED A GOOD PACE DESPITE HIS INJURY. **SILENT**. NO ATTEMPTS TO **CONVINCE** US OF ANYTHING.

THE ONE TIME OUR EYES MET, HIS **BEGGED**. TO LET GO? FORGET ABOUT THE THINGS HE HADN'T REVEALED?

THE DOOR UP TO BILL'S OFFICE WAS STILL OPEN. **SOMEONE** HAD TURNED ON THE LIGHTS.

YOU FIRST, TOM. SMOOTH AND **QUIET**. ROBIN—I'LL LET YOU KNOW WHEN IT'S SAFE TO COME UP WITH BILL.

THE GARDENER, CARL SLEET... THE MAN WHOSE VOICE HAD DRAWN BEN TO THE PARK IN THE MIDDLE OF THE NIGHT.

TIED WITH ZIP TIES, COP-STYLE. **HAYGOOD**? NO. CREEDMAN LOOKED AS **SURPRISED** AS WE WERE.

DON'T **SHOOT**. NOW, HOW 'BOUT I MOVE **MY** SCUMBAG OUT OF THE WAY SO YOU CAN GET **YOUR** SCUMBAG THROUGH?

MY GUN IS OVER THERE ON THE DESK.

I HEARD SHOTS. EVERYONE *OKAY*? WHERE ARE ROBIN AND DR. MORELAND?

THEY'RE *WAITING* FOR ME TO GIVE THE ALL CLEAR. BILL'S WOUNDED.

DON'T WORRY. IT'S *GENUINE*. EXCEPT FOR THE NAME. IT'S ACTUALLY JANE BENDIG: DEFENSE DEPARTMENT SENIOR INVESTIGATOR.

I UNDERSTAND YOU BEING WARY, BUT IF I *WANTED* TO SHOOT YOU, YOU'D *ALREADY* BE DEAD.

JO PICKER.

YOU HAVE A GUN. MINE IS WAY OVER THERE. I'M NO *THREAT*, ALEX.

NOW...WHY DON'T YOU GIVE YOUR FRIENDS THE WORD SO WE CAN GET ALL THIS SETTLED?

THAT ARM NEEDS **ATTENTION,** DOCTOR.

IT WILL BE **FINE.** NOTHING A—

CARL?

I'VE BEEN WATCHING CARL FOR A LONG TIME NOW. HE'S BEEN A **VERY** NAUGHTY BOY.

*"PILFERING DR. MORELAND'S OLD SURGICAL KIT. PUTTING **COCKROACHES** IN PEOPLE'S ROOMS."*

"TONIGHT HE WAS SKULKING AROUND, WATCHING AS YOU FOUND THE TUNNEL."

"HE CALLED HIS BUDDIES AS SOON AS YOU TWO WENT DOWN."

I'LL TAKE CUSTODY OF **YOUR** SCUMBAG NOW.

ALL THESE YEARS, CARL'S BEEN HOLDING A *GRUDGE* AGAINST YOU, DOC.

SOMETHING ABOUT A *COUSIN* WHO SAW A MONSTER AND DIED OF A HEART ATTACK.

"SAYS *YOU* TREATED THE GUY. *LIED* TO HIM AND WITHHELD MEDICATION."

"THAT'S HIS *EXCUSE*, ANYWAY. I'M SURE THE *MONEY* THEY PAID HIM DIDN'T HURT, EITHER."

YOU DON'T HAVE TO *CONVINCE* ME, DOC.

I HEARD A LOT OF *SHOTS*. ANY OF THEM GO INTO HAYGOOD?

THAT'S NOT *TRUE*. HIS ARTERIES WERE CLOGGED. HIGHLY ADVANCED ATHERO—

YEAH... FIVE OF THEM.

FOR A SPLIT SECOND THERE WAS SOMETHING PERSONAL IN HER EXPRESSION. HAYGOOD MONKEYING WITH LYMAN'S PLANE?

NOTHING WORSE THAN A BAD COP.

YOUR HUSBAND...DID HAYGOOD **CAUSE** THE—

YEAH, BUT LYMAN WASN'T MY **HUSBAND.** THOUGH WE DID HAVE A... **RELATIONSHIP.**

HE WASN'T DEFENSE DEPARTMENT. JUST KEEPING ME COMPANY.

I **TRIED** TALKING HIM OUT OF FLYING IN THAT HEAP...

ANYWAY, LET'S GET THESE **MORONS** SOMEWHERE SAFE AND SEE TO THAT WOUNDED ARM.

WHAT DO YOU KEEP DOWN THERE IN THAT TUNNEL, DR. M.?

YOU CAN **TELL** ME. I'M ONE OF THE **GOOD GUYS.**

IT'S...A VERY **LONG** STORY.

WE LOCKED CREEDMAN AND SLEET IN CLOSETS IN THE BASEMENT. ROBIN FOUND PAM, AND TOLD HER TO BRING HER MEDICAL KIT TO THE HOME'S FRONT ROOM.

OH, DADDY.

I'M ALL RIGHT, KITTEN.

CLEAN THROUGH THE LATISSIMUS. NO ARTERIAL DAMAGE.

JO WANTED TO KNOW EVERYTHING ABOUT OUR TRIP INTO THE TUNNELS. I TOLD HER.

SHE'D BEEN WELL-TRAINED TO MAINTAIN HER COMPOSURE, BUT SHE WAS PALE BY THE TIME I FINISHED.

ALEX, ROBIN... COULD I HAVE A MINUTE WITH YOU IN THE LIVING ROOM?

UNBELIEVABLE. SIX OF THEM...DOWN THERE ALL THESE YEARS? THEIR EXISTENCE ALONE COULD BLOW THE LID OFF THIS THING.

ARE YOU INVESTIGATING HOFFMAN, OR STASHER-LAYMAN AS A WHOLE?

LET'S JUST SAY WE'VE BEEN WORKING ON THIS FOR A LONG TIME.

CORRUPTION. KICKBACKS. MAJOR FINANCIAL ANGLE...THE KIND OF THING THAT RAISES EVERYONE'S TAXES A FEW BUCKS, BUT NO ONE EVER HEARS ABOUT.

I'VE GOT TO SEE THEM. WHEN-EVER DOCTOR BILL IS WELL ENOUGH TO TAKE ME DOWN I'LL—

HIS WHOLE PURPOSE HAS BEEN TO SHELTER THEM. HE'S NOT GOING TO USE THEM.

I ADMIRE HIS PRINCIPLES, BUT THINGS CHANGE. YOU HAVE TO ADAPT.

DR. MORELAND... WHENEVER YOU'RE **READY**, I NEED YOU TO TAKE ME TO SEE WHAT YOU HAVE DOWN THERE.

HE'S NOT GOING ANY-WHERE.

IT'S SOMETHING OF AN **EMERGENCY**. A LOT'S AT STAKE. **RIGHT**, DOCTOR?

JO...WHO THE HELL **ARE** YOU?

LONG STORY. COME WITH ME FOR A SEC.

I'M NOT LEAVING HIM **ALONE**.

PLEASE...GO WITH HER, KITTEN. FOR MY SAKE.

ROBIN, COULD YOU GO ALONG AND HELP **EXPLAIN** THINGS?

EVENTUALLY, JO AND ROBIN WERE ABLE TO LEAD PAM AWAY. I DIDN'T HAVE TO IMAGINE HOW SHE'D FEEL IN A FEW MINUTES, AS ALL HER FATHER'S **LIES** UNFOLDED AROUND HER.

YOUR **QUESTIONS** DOWN THERE, ALEX... ABOUT WHAT HOFFMAN HAS OVER ME. THERE'S SOME **TRUTH** TO THEM.

I WAS A **DIFFERENT** MAN THEN, ALEX. WOMEN...**HAVING** THEM...MEANT SO MUCH TO ME.

I KNOW. DENNIS IS YOUR **SON**, ISN'T HE?

HOW DID YOU—?

I COULDN'T GET OVER HOW YOU REACTED TO **PAM** BEING WITH **DENNIS**. YOU DON'T STRIKE ME AS A RACIST, SO **WHY** THE VEHEMENCE?

THEN, WITH WHAT CREEDMAN SAID... IT JUST **CLICKED** INTO PLACE.

AS A FATHER, I'M A **DISGRACE**. THEY'VE **BOTH** TURNED OUT BETTER THAN I DESERVE.

I TOLD MYSELF I WAS SENDING PAM AWAY FROM THE ISLAND FOR HER OWN GOOD. **HOGWASH**. I COULDN'T STAND THE GUILT. OVER JACQUI... AND **OTHERS**.

THAT **BASTARD** CREEDMAN WAS RIGHT. I WAS A REPUGNANT LECHER. I DID SERVE AS MY OWN ABORTIONIST. JACQUI REFUSED TO TERMINATE.

POOR **BARBARA**...SHE HAD NEVER BEEN A HAPPY WOMAN. I MADE HER **MISERABLE**.

IT WAS THE **BABY** THAT DROVE BARBARA TO SUICIDE. THE FACT THAT I'D ACTUALLY LET IT GET **THAT** FAR...

HOW DID SHE FIND OUT? HOFFMAN?

I NEVER WAS VERY **DISCREET**. HE FOUND OUT, AND TOLD HER ABOUT IT IN HAWAII... JUST TO **WOUND** ME.

THE NEXT MORNING, SHE **WALKED** INTO THE OCEAN.

THAT'S THE HOLD HE HAS OVER ME: KEEPING IT A SECRET FROM PAM.

I **KILLED** HER MOTHER, AND SO DID HE. IN THAT SENSE WE **ARE** PARTNERS. RAMS LOCKING HORNS, JUST AS YOU SAID.

A BEAUTIFUL ANALOGY, MY FRIEND. ARE YOU **OFFENDED** BY MY THINKING OF YOU AS A **FRIEND**?

NO, BILL. YOU **HAVE** TO TELL PAM.

SHE'LL **DESPISE** ME.

SHE **LOVES** YOU. SHE WANTS TO GET CLOSER TO YOU. ONCE SHE REALIZES THE GOOD THINGS YOU'VE DONE, SHE'LL BE WILLING TO—

BILL...?

TIME **DECEIVES**. **TERRIBLE** THINGS I'VE DONE, SON. ALL THE **TERRIBLE** THINGS...

THREE DAYS LATER, ROBIN AND I WERE SOAKING UP ALL THE *CIVILIZATION* WE COULD GET IN A LUXURY SUITE IN HAWAII.

WE ORDERED ROOM SERVICE AND READ EVERY NEWSPAPER AND MAGAZINE WE COULD GET OUR HANDS ON.

IN A BANQUET HALL DOWNSTAIRS, SENATOR HOFFMAN WAS UNVEILING HIS *BOLD*, NEW INITIATIVE. A BANNER READ, "PACIFIC RIM PROGRESS: A NEW DAWN."

BIG NEWS. BIG ENOUGH TO BE TELEVISED ACROSS THE ISLANDS.

HERE HE GOES.

THE SENATOR'S TRADEMARK SMILE. A ONE-LINER. PAUSE FOR THE LAUGHTER. *THEN...*

THEN, SOMETHING *CHANGED* IN HIS EYES. I MIGHT NOT HAVE NOTICED IF I HADN'T BEEN LOOKING FOR IT.

A SHUTTER-SNAP FLICKER OF *CONFUSION.*

JO/JANE HAD BEEN WORKING *NONSTOP* THE LAST THREE DAYS, USING CREEDMAN'S COMPUTER TO SEND BOGUS MESSAGES HAD BEEN THE EASY PART.

CONVINCING MORELAND HE COULD *REDEEM* HIMSELF HAD BEEN FAR MORE CHALLENGING. GETTING THE "KIDS" EXAMINED BY DOCTORS, TALKING TO BILL ABOUT MORALITY, *ABSOLUTION.* IN THE END, SHE WORE HIM DOWN.

HOFFMAN SEEMED TO BE ORDERING THOSE AROUND HIM TO MOVE...*TO STOP THE INTRUSION.*

MORE DARK-SUITED MEN APPEARED AROUND BILL AND JO/JILL, FLASHING **BADGES** AND RESTRAINING HOFFMAN'S MEN.

GASPS FROM THE ROOM. SOMEONE SAID, "*MY GOD!*" A GLASS DROPPED AND SHATTERED ON THE GRANITE FLOOR.

MY NAME IS WOODROW WILSON MORELAND. I'M A DOCTOR. I HAVE A **STORY** TO TELL.

ACROSS THE CROWDED FLOOR OF THE BANQUET HALL, HOFFMAN FINALLY **STOPPED** SMILING.

A FEW DAYS LATER WE WERE ON THE PLANE BACK TO L.A. FIRST CLASS, COURTESY OF THE DEFENSE DEPARTMENT.

I WOKE FROM A CHABLIS-INDUCED NAP, SUDDENLY THINKING ABOUT *HAYGOOD*. WHO HE'D BEEN AS A CHILD. WAS THERE A MOTHER SOMEWHERE WHO WOULD *MOURN* HIM?

STUPID THOUGHTS, BUT INEVITABLE. I TRIED TO SHAKE MYSELF OUT OF IT, THINKING ABOUT THE *GOOD* I'D BEEN PART OF.

BEN *FREED*. SOME LIMITED *HOPE* FOR ARUK.

THE *"KIDS"* LIBERATED AND WELL CARED FOR. MORELAND HOSPITALIZED, TOO, AND EVALUATED.

NO ALZHEIMER'S. JUST AN *EXHAUSTED* OLD MAN.

HE STILL HADN'T TOLD PAM OR DENNIS. HOLDING BACK, AS HE HAD BEEN FOR THREE DECADES.

HE'D *REINVENTED* HIMSELF. GONE FROM A CRUEL WOMANIZER TO THE PATRON SAINT OF ARUK. BUT YET HE FELT *GUILTY*. OTHER SINS?

AS WE'D LEFT HIS HOSPITAL ROOM, HE CALLED OUT, *"TIME DECEIVES"* AGAIN. ANOTHER *CONFESSION?*

MY MIND SETTLED ON THE *ONE* CASE WE'D DISCUSSED THAT HADN'T BEEN PART OF THE "PARADISE NEEDLE" OR MORELAND'S BATTLES WITH HOFFMAN.

THE "CAT-WOMAN."

MORE *SUBTERFUGE*? PAM'S CHEATING HUSBAND HAD HURT HER SO DEEPLY...HAD HURT MORELAND'S "KITTEN."

THE HUSBAND'S CHEST *CRUSHED* IN A FREAK ACCIDENT. BILL SAID THE "CAT-WOMAN'S" HUSBAND HAD DIED, HIS CHEST *RAVAGED* BY CANCER.

COULD BILL HAVE *ENGINEERED* THE DEATH, AND FED ME A STORY TO HINT AT IT? "TERRIBLE THINGS," HE'D SAID. "TIME DECEIVES."

I'D NEVER KNOW. WHY DID I *CARE*? MAYBE ONE DAY, I WOULDN'T.

COMFY, DOCTOR?

YES. FINE... THANKS.

SAD ABOUT THE END OF YOUR VACATION?

NO. I'M READY TO GET BACK TO REALITY.

—END—

JONATHAN KELLERMAN is one of the world's most popular authors. He has brought his expertise as a clinical psychologist to more than thirty bestselling crime novels, including the Alex Delaware series, *The Butcher's Theater*, *Billy Straight*, *The Conspiracy Club*, *Twisted*, and *True Detectives*. With his wife, the novelist Faye Kellerman, he coauthored the bestsellers *Double Homicide* and *Capital Crimes*. He is the author of numerous essays, short stories, scientific articles, two children's books, and three volumes of psychology, including *Savage Spawn: Reflections on Violent Children*, as well as the lavishly illustrated *With Strings Attached: The Art and Beauty of Vintage Guitars*. He has won the Goldwyn, Edgar, and Anthony awards and has been nominated for a Shamus Award. Jonathan and Faye Kellerman live in California, New Mexico, and New York. Their four children include the novelists Jesse Kellerman and Aliza Kellerman.

After a long career as a comic book artist, **ANDE PARKS** has become a full-time writer in recent years. His writing credits include the graphic novels *Union Station* and *Capote in Kansas*. The latter was named a Notable Book for the state of Kansas in 2006, the first graphic novel to receive such an honor.

Ande currently writes *The Green Hornet* and *The Lone Ranger* monthly comics for Dynamite Press. He is also developing new graphic novel projects. Ande lives in Baldwin City, Kansas, with his lovely wife and two children. He enjoys crime fiction, golf, vintage fedoras, and a nice glass of bourbon.

Illustrator, painter, and printmaker **MICHAEL GAYDOS**'s list of credits includes illustrations, graphic novels, and sequential artwork for Marvel, DC, NBC, Dark Horse, Image, IDW, Top Cow, Fox Atomic, Virgin, Tundra, NBM, Caliber, and White Wolf, among others. He has received two Eisner Award nominations for his work on *Alias* with Brian Michael Bendis for Marvel. Michael's fine artwork has also been the subject of a number of solo exhibitions the past few years and his work is collected worldwide.